Praise for The Great Molinas

Jack Molinas was the quintessential amoral hero of our time, and his story has been begging to be told. Well, it finally has been told, and superbly, by Neil Isaacs. He has done it the best and most meaningful way by turning it into a novel in which he and his dark angel intersect on a series of pivotal levels. No writer could possibly have invented Jack Molinas, but Isaacs has re-invented him with skill, courage, and an artfully sustained intensity.

Irvin Faust, author of The Steagle

I couldn't turn the pages fast enough. Neil Isaacs has produced a powerful profile of a sport original, a fascinating study of a complicated man with enormous talent and strange personality

Mort Olshan, editor/publisher of The Gold Sheet

…a very scary book that will make you sweat. Neil Isaacs has captured all the divertse personalities of one of the greatest basketball players and gamblers to ever play at both games. It reads like fiction. The scary part being that it's true.

Chet Forte. late producer of ABC's Monday Night Football

The spellbinding story of the legendary Jack Molinas is more than a court-long shot at the buzzer, and Neil Isaacs tells it with the depth and feeling it deserves. Unlike the many ways this novel could have been handled, Isaacs does it as a narrative that investigates itself—and its teller—even as Molinas's fascinating tale is told. To some extent every good writer becomes his subject, and that happens here. The Great Molinas is a novel about basketball and everything else, too.

Jerry Klinkowitz, author of The Short Season

Also by Neil D. Isaacs

The Great Molinas

The Miller Masks: A Novel in Stories

The Doaker's Story

Fated to Fail: Tales from a Marriage

The Man Who Touched Billie and Other Stories

Flirtations with Fame: Memoirs of a Celebrity Manqué

The Package and the Baggage: Help for Couples and Their Counselors

You Bet Your Life: The Burdens of Gambling

The Triumph of Artifice: Studies in 20th-Century Narrative

The Queen Must Live: Mythical Patterns of Royalty, Sexuality, and Mortality

Jock Culture, U.S.A.

Fiction into Film (with Rachel Maddux and Stirling Silliphant)

All the Moves: A History of College Basketball

Sports Illustrated Basketball (with Dick Motta)

Vintage NBA: The Pioneer Era

Innocence and Wonder: Baseball through the Eyes of Batboys

Batboys and the World of Baseball

Grace Paley: A Study of the Short Fiction

Covering the Spread (with Gerald Strine)

Checking Back: A History of the National Hockey League

Eudora Welty

Structural Principles in Old English Poetry

One Thing
and Another
and Other
Stories

Neil D. Isaacs

ARCHWAY
PUBLISHING

Archway Publishing books may be ordered through booksellers or by contacting:

Archway Publishing
1663 Liberty Drive
Bloomington, IN 47403
www.archwaypublishing.com
1 (888) 242-5904

ISBN: 978-1-4808-4841-2 (sc)
ISBN: 978-1-4808-4842-9 (hc)
ISBN: 978-1-4808-4843-6 (e)

Library of Congress Control Number: 2017908980

Print information available on the last page.

Archway Publishing rev. date: 7/6/2017

Dedication

To David, Mickey, Anna, Marjorie,
Sarah, Jessie, Ilana, Adam,
Jacob, Makaela. Xavier, and Damian

For a proud and loving grandpa to be remembered

Contents

The Man Who Touched Billie

Three times I saw him, three times all told in thirty years. And yet I felt that I knew him, perhaps as well as I sensed he knew me.

The first time was when I was sixteen, the summer before my junior year in high school. That spring, my brother was home from winning the war. He had marched across much of Europe with Patton's Third Army, and he never talked about it at home. For weeks at a time he'd be out drinking with his buddies every night, and I rarely saw him. And then, for a day or two, he'd hang out with me in the afternoons and evenings, recapturing the kind of closeness we used to have when the big brother would entertain and challenge the kid by inventing and playing games with me for hours at a time.

These periodic swings hardly made a difference to me, focused as I was on two things. Trying to get close to this or that girl and scheming to find ways to practice my driving. My brother had won a lot of money shooting craps on the troop ship coming home, and he had bought an old LaSalle coupe with some of it. Once in a while he let me practice with it, and erratic and trouble-prone as the car was I loved the way it held the road and cornered at high speed.

For us growing up in New Haven in those days, nights out—whether with dates or just in a crowd, after a movie or party or ballgame—ended up in one of two ways. Down to Wooster Street for apizz' at Sally's or Pepe's, with the obligatory drive by to see the Old

Lady of Pitkin Alley sitting eternally in her second-story bedroom window, or out Derby Avenue to the Bowl Spa for lobster rolls. There had to be a car and driver, and sometimes my brother provided both. I remember once when I had a date with Stephanie Simanski and the brakes failed in the LaSalle on the way to the dance. My brother had to downshift and use the parking brake to get to a stop. It was a harrowing ride—and that was the only date I ever got with the lovely Stephanie.

I had barely seen my brother for a couple of weeks when he woke me up on a morning in early July and said, "Get ready, we're going to Newport."

Even more exciting than the prospect of going to the Jazz Festival where many of my favorite performers would be appearing was the thrill of going on such a jaunt with my brother. The hours on the road and at the site passed in a heady blur, the drive and the music producing a kind of enchanted buzz that I could re-experience in succeeding years only by artificial means. The music was great and it was great to be there, but I couldn't say without looking it up who was playing or what they played. Except for Lady Day.

In those days, the stage was set up at the crest of a green rise, just two or two and a half feet off the ground. There was nothing like the kind of security you find at concerts now, and of course the sound system was primitive. There were hundreds of folding chairs ranged in uneven rows, but this was a jazz extravaganza and no one was sitting during sets. We had worked our way right up to the front of the stage when Billie came on, and we stood enthralled by a sustained intensity of vocal artistry. Her range of emotional deliveries, her spontaneously creative phrasing, her playful manipulation of rhythms, were all overwhelming. And it was all enhanced by my appreciation, mirroring my brother's fascination, of the powerful physical beauty of the woman, the gardenia in her hair, the large-boned suppleness of her body, the profound originality of her haunted eyes and regal features.

The ovation at the end of her set was enormous, climbing up the slope at us in waves, and Billie came forward to acknowledge it. And toppled from the stage.

The man caught her. Not broke her fall, but caught her in his arms, a shock in itself because he seemed to be smaller than she was. He was wearing a suit, summer-weight of that nondescript solid color that might have been gray or olive, and in that way was exceptional in a crowd of shorts-and-polo-shirted fans. His shoulders were broad and his belly flat, but he seemed to lack the solidity and strength implied by his shape and his action. I thought he might be a few years older than my brother.

What struck me most were his eyes and the look on his face. We were no more than eight or ten feet apart. I could have reached out and touched them, and as it happened, almost in slow motion, we made eye contact. I'm sure of it. His jaw was set, there was grim determination in his face, his lips just slightly open in flat lines across his mouth. But in his eyes were amazed exhilaration and the radiance of ecstatic epiphany.

What he saw in my face, mouth agape and eyes popped into stunned globes, was awe that was more like the fear of stumbling into awareness from the dimness of naiveté. Much later I realized that Lady Day was drunk or high. I had turned toward them as she fell, and my brother tapped me on the shoulder from behind.

"Let's go," he said, his tone flat but with a touch of grumble to it. "There's no more for us here, nothing to top that."

The second time was eight years later, during my abortive graduate school days in Boston. I was living in one of those elegant brownstones on the river side of Beacon that had been broken up into apartments, splitting the rent three ways with a law student who studied day and night and a med student who was rarely there. I was there too much, with time on my hands now that I had stopped going to classes, reading for pleasure since I had quit studying books for grades and papers.

My brother was back in Europe, trying to learn how to be a painter, mostly in Spain, where the living was easier on the Costa Brava, the light and colors more palatable to his palette, and the memories of his time in Belgium and Luxembourg and Germany and Czechoslovakia and especially France far enough removed to be tolerable. Our parents had retreated into a cocoon of a smaller apartment, preparing to isolate themselves for the onset of old age, but still willing to support me for a while until I "found myself," just as they were subsidizing my brother's artistic apprenticeship. And the girl of my dreams/nightmares had broken up with me yet again, to "explore other options," in the phrase that gave me fits of anxiety.

More than three years of on-and-off coupling had worn me out, my moods swinging between the elation of "Them There Eyes" and the despair of "Gloomy Sunday." Always there was a soundtrack of Billie's to underscore and interpret the situation.

Billie Holiday had lost her cabaret license to perform in New York, but George Wein had booked her into his Storyville club in Boston for a week, and I was there every night, sipping scotch and milk. He had put together a quartet of young musicians, proud to accompany her, with no New York career to put at risk by playing with her, and they were good. They gave her a steady beat to play around with, a subdued melody for her to play against with her still startling harmonies, and the call-and-response arrangements she had perfected with Teddy Wilson.

Tuesday night was a triumph, all the critics on their feet, their reviews the next day full of exuberant praise. The club was packed all week, and I never missed a set. As early as the second show Wednesday night, I noticed changes. She'd drag behind the beat a little more than was right, almost a caricature of her style, and the reading of the lyric would stumble on occasion. Over the next two nights, this progressed into slurrings of both words and tunes that were still striking but now seemed self-destructive.

The first set on Saturday was a disaster. "Ain't Nobody's Bidness" was a shambles and the classic sophistication of her "Miss Brown to You" arrangement had become a senseless misinterpretation—or more like non-interpretation. The group didn't know how to handle it, whether to try to follow with changes in beat and key or be more insistent about keeping her on her marks. She closed, as always, with her own "Strange Fruit," and the horrifying power of the lyric was incoherent to anyone who wasn't familiar with it.

She looked worn, defeated, frightened, yet still hauntingly beautiful. The whole house, it seemed, held its breath as she staggered off stage and wound her way along the darkest aisles back to the bar. When she made it, there was a collective sigh of relief that she hadn't fallen. Her manager was sitting there, two stools down from me, and she stood in front of him, legs spread for balance, as she leaned toward him and said something about going out for a walk and a breath of air.

Suddenly the man was there, holding her coat. He helped her into it and held his arm out. She took it, without once looking at him, and they left the building. He looked the same, wearing another nondescript plain-colored suit. I watched them through the glass door of the club and winced when I saw him close his right hand over hers as she held his left arm, but she seemed to be walking more steadily now. Her manager shrugged back to his beer and I avoided looking at him, but I was the one who waited nervously for them to come back.

When they did, Billie was smiling that unearthly glow of hers, and I could see that she would get through her other set. But I wasn't going to stay around for it. I made eye contact with the man. He never registered recognition, but I saw him clearly now. He had aged more than a decade, I thought, but well, with added heft to him or what I could only think of as substance. There was strength of character there, a knowing look of experience and endurance, and a solidity of satisfaction that came with that self-contained strength.

⊂━━━○━━━⊃

Twenty-two years later, almost to the week, I was in Phoenix at the end of what was supposed to be a period of recovery and planning. I was between marriages, which had its mixture of feelings: loneliness and regret, excitement and freedom. To complicate things, I was also between jobs, contemplating a total change of career and relocation. There were some opportunities in Seattle, but I was thinking maybe Vancouver. My brother was in St. Paul, jack-of-all-trades for a small ad agency, staying out of the cold, reining in his bachelor's taste for minor luxuries. Our parents were ten and eight years gone to Connecticut graves we rarely visited.

I had planned a solitary fortnight, a time for getting away but also getting ready to make the choices and sort out the stresses, anxieties, challenges, and temptations that went with them. The first week was in Aruba, where I had latched onto a junket despite the fact that my gambling was the low-roller type that didn't deserve getting comped for room and board at any self-respecting casino. I spent far fewer hours at the tables than under the divi-divi trees, and the highlight of the week was seeing the flock of wild parakeets roosting at sunset in the side of the highest cliff on the island and hearing their unearthly noise subsiding into silence.

Then I had three days in San Antonio, having some great meals along River Walk, taking the obligatory tour of the Alamo, and buying, at a bargain-basement price, a handsome pair of hand-tooled cowboy boots at the Lucchese factory showroom. And now I had three days at a modest Arizona resort that I had picked because they advertised a number of running trails through "desert gardens." So I had done my running in the mornings and caught some spring training ballgames later in the day.

My last night I decided to get out of standard tourist territory, and I put on my Luccheses and walked into a part of town where ordinary blue-collar and cowboy-hatted Americans hung out. No retirees here. I followed the weathered faces of an older couple into a Mexican restaurant, finding that it was essentially a bar that offered standard Tex-Mex fare at a fraction of what I had seen on glitzy menus elsewhere.

The bar, which occupied fully a quarter of the space, was crowded for the early evening hour, and I took a booth more than halfway down the opposite side, indicating that I wanted dinner. I sat facing away from the door, to cut down somewhat on the conversational hum from the bar, and found myself looking up at a bright shiny Wurlitzer that dominated the whole back of the room. I ordered my first Tecate and walked to the machine, hoping to find some Willie Nelson or Roy Orbison, maybe even a Freddy Fender or Gloria Estefan I could tolerate among the welter of current country-western I expected.

This was one of those big old machines with a hundred ninety-two 45's (sets of 24 numbered under headings A through H), and it was a revelation. I thought I had died and gone to jukebox heaven. I could hardly believe what I was seeing, stepped back, and looked around the place to see if the clientele was anything but what my first impression had taken in. The offerings simply did not fit either the ambience or the demographics.

The first item that registered was Wynonie Harris and that pre rock-and-roll r. and b. classic, "Everybody's Rockin' Tonight," among a score of such numbers. Ivory Joe Hunter was there with "Since I Met You, Baby" and Nellie Lutcher all excited about her "Real Gone Guy." There were some rare early blues recordings, including Robert Johnson himself, Bessie Smith too. There were blues singers with big bands, Jimmy Rushing and Joe Williams (on Basie's "Cherry Red" arrangement). There was Al Hibbler on Ellington's "Do Nothin' Till You Hear from Me." Cootie Williams was there, fronting his own group, Jimmy Lunceford ditto, and Jack Teagarden to boot. There was the first set of Slim and Slam covers, a pair of songs with Jackie Cain and Roy Kral that I didn't even know they'd recorded, and several Coltrane and Johnny Hartman duets.

And that wasn't the half of it. Most of the selections were female vocalists, more than a hundred songs by singers I had grown up revering, voices that had taken me and accompanied me through all the inexpressible passages of my life. Whoever had chosen this menu had the kind of comprehensively eclectic taste I stood in awe of. Assembled there were Mabel Mercer, the inimitable café stylist, and Chippy Hill, greatest of the shout singers, Dinah Washington, who reinvented vocal blues slides, and Lee Wiley, one sweet bitch of a singer, as George Frazier once called her in liner notes.

And Billie. Four dozen Billie Holiday recordings, from every period with every accompanying artist she'd ever shared a studio or live recording date with. I emptied all the change in my pocket into the machine. I hit half a dozen of my favorites, records that had some specific memories associated with them, and then lined up a dozen by Billie to follow those warm-up acts. I knew I was in for a long evening. It was as if you opened up the TV Guide and found every movie you loved listed and you knew there'd be no sleeping that week.

I sat back down in my booth, ordered the combination platter and another Tecate, though I was tempted by an item on the menu called "Pepe's Mexican Pizza," which set off memories of my teen years in New Haven. I had been struggling for two weeks or more trying to focus on the future, and here this music was driving me deep into the past, exhilarating and depressing at the same time. Tears long repressed seemed to be cresting for a fall.

It was during the second of my Lady Day choices that he appeared. I remember that it was precisely at the end of the first chorus. "Ooh, ooh, ooh, what a little moonlight can do-oo-oo," Billie sang as he walked past my booth straight to the jukebox. He was wearing wrinkled khakis and an unbuttoned cotton cardigan over a faded denim shirt. He studied the selections on deck and then looked around to see who might have picked them. He was old, paunchy, and shorter, as if gravity had pulled him down an inch or two and left the excess weight at his beltline. His hair was mostly gone, the thick brown of it replaced by a fringe of dull gray at the temples and back. The creases in his face were deep and the eyes seemed care-worn but still with a kind of earnest brightness. I would have known him anywhere.

Those eyes fixed on mine and his expression of concern seemed to lighten. A smile played around the corners of his mouth, and he nodded once in my direction. We never spoke, but that knowing nod was worth three thousand words. Here they are.

Collared

Ever since he moved out of the house, Wednesday had become Simon's favorite day of the week. It wasn't the only time he saw Leni—other afternoons he drove her to soccer practice, and she spent parts of most weekends in his apartment, usually after soccer games. But piano-lesson days were different because they went out to dinner afterwards.

Counting the phone calls during the week, they seemed to have more time for each other now. Still, there was no sense of urgency or intimacy about it. They would talk superficially about school, friends, sports, music, sometimes a little politics, but the silences between the topics felt comfortable, too.

Simon had determined never to ask her anything about her mother, though of course he would have wanted to know. It was just that if Leni was having any problems with their arrangement he didn't want to add a conflict of loyalties. He trusted her to let him know anything he should know, and he took the absence of reports as a comforting sign of the absence of trouble.

As usual that late spring afternoon, he picked her up after school, drove her home, hung out in the house looking over some work he'd brought with him while she did her homework, and then drove her to Mrs. Copelan's. He sat in the "other" room while Leni worked on her two pieces, a Schubert etude and "Stairway to Heaven," hearing the sound of the woman's voice as she made her comments but unable to make out the actual words. He liked it that way, never wanting to interfere with Leni's learning process, but listening to her playing. Once again he sensed that she was more fully engaged with the classical piece though it was popular music she claimed to prefer—something else he never mentioned to her.

When she finished, Simon's appreciative grin was as much for her appearance as for her playing. Whether because Mrs. Copelan expected it or because they were going out to dinner, Leni always wore a skirt, blouse, and sweater to piano, rather than the usual jeans, sweats or shorts. She always looked good to him in the most casual or careless get-up, but he loved the plaid pleated skirt she had on that day, the Peter Pan collar of the plain white shirt, and the dark green cardigan—his Wednesday Leni at her brown-eyed prettiest.

They sat through the usual Italian fare and the usual chitchat with the usual silences, the usual comfortable sense that everything was okay, and he drove her home as usual about eight-thirty. Simon watched her go up the path and through the side door before driving away. He hadn't gotten out of the development, no more than two and a half blocks, when it hit him that something was wrong. He made a quick u-turn and headed back before consciously registering what it was. He hadn't seen a car in the carport. With the so-called Grove Lake rapist committing his random attacks in the county, most of them home invasions, this was not a time for a fourteen-year-old girl to be left at home alone.

No more than four minutes had passed but he was convinced that the Grove Lake rapist was in the house with his precious Leni. It was not just the passing flash of fantasized calamity that he, like most parents, often experienced when apart from their children, but an uncanny uncertainty. And he flipped automatically into his crisis mode, a paradoxical state of clarity and calm that served him well in his volunteer role on the suicide hotline at the Crisis Center.

He drove slowly past the house, making out two distinct, separate shadows behind the drawn curtains. The rapist's m.o. had been thoroughly reported, and Simon knew he had just a few minutes before Leni would be led or forced upstairs to her own bedroom. Still, he coolly considered that if he burst right in, the bastard would get away, as he had on two other occasions when surprised by a third party.

He pulled into the Calabresi driveway across the street, and Pete, the world's best neighbor, opened the door before Simon could ring the bell.

"Call 9-1-1, Pete. Tell them the rapist is in my house and to close off the area. I'm gonna chase him out, but I don't want him getting away this time."

"Wait, Si. Let me get you a weapon."

"No," he said. No one knew whether this guy was ever actually armed, and Simon didn't want any shooting in the house with Leni there.

He moved quickly and quietly, breathing steadily, up to the side door. The shapes behind the curtains told him they were still on the ground floor but the space between them had closed. He put his key in the lock, quieted his breath to be sure his voice sounded normal when he called out, not alarmed or threatening. He counted to five, then shoved the door open heavily so that it banged against the washer, and used the tired old joke of greeting.

"Hi, honey, I'm home. Where are you?" When he came around the corner into the living room, Leni was standing still, halfway up the stairs, the front door was open, and the rapist was gone.

Leni wasn't crying or even trembling, and he ran up to her and hugged her close. They walked back down together, to shut and lock the door, and when they looked out there was the Grove Lake rapist, face down on the path, his ski mask still on, his hands behind his back, no weapon in sight—except for the shotgun in Pete Calabresi's hands.

Simon had heard nothing of it, but he instantly imagined the quick barking command and the immediate surrender in the face of clear authority. Looking at the tableau out there, he took in what must have impressed the guy most powerfully, that in addition to the double barrels staring him down, the holder of that weapon also had his service revolver tucked into his belt but in plain intimidating view.

No more than three minutes later, the police had the rapist in custody. Over and over, Simon and Leni repeated the formulaic exchange: "Are you all right?" and "I'm okay, Daddy." Finally, sitting in the kitchen, she with her Diet Coke and he with his ice water, he said, still struggling to keep the storming emotions out of his voice, "Where's your mother?"

"I don't know."

The way she hung her head as she said it stopped any follow-up. Embarrassed or ashamed for her mother, uncomfortable with where his question was heading? He didn't know, didn't need to know, not then. He hugged her again, and the scene was broken by the arrival of the police lieutenant who was heading up the task force, just a minute or two behind the first responders. He wanted them to come down to the station to make their statements, but Simon asked if they could do it right there, that he didn't want Leni to have to leave the house.

Lt. Harper said it was fine with him, they'd just have to wait till an assistant district attorney got there. While they waited, father and daughter sat on the piano bench, she lightly running through some ten-finger exercises, he with his arm lightly around her. When the prosecutor arrived, Simon gave his version first, telling the story of their evening and including, minimally, the background detail of the trial separation and the custodial arrangements. Harper said nothing, nor did A.D.A. Lopez, her eyes focused on Leni the whole time, a kind of neutral-trying-to-be-concerned look on her face.

Harper took notes, giving Simon a quizzical look when he got to the part about going first to Pete's house. "You're lucky to have a neighbor like Calabresi" was all he said before turning to Leni, and then Simon heard for the first time what had happened in those terrible minutes from when he dropped her off until he burst back in.

"Why did you let him into the house?"

"My dad had just dropped me off. I thought, like, he had forgotten something or there was something he wanted to tell me, so I opened the door when he knocked and he just, like, walked in, didn't even have to push."

"Doesn't your dad have a key?"

"The only key we use is to the side door. Even if I had thought about it I'd have thought he was, like, in a hurry or whatever. But he had just left and I didn't think it could be anyone else."

"You didn't scream? Weren't you frightened by the mask?"

"I was more, like, surprised. But I knew right away who it was."

"You recognized him?"

"No, I mean, I knew it was the guy that was doing all that stuff—it's all over the TV."

"What did he say to you?"

"He's like, 'I don't wanna hurt you,' and I'm like, 'Well, that's good because I don't want you to hurt me.'"

"Didn't you think about running out the door?"

"By the time I thought of it he had shut it and was standing too close to it."

"Did he show you a weapon?"

"No."

"Did you think he had one?"

"I really didn't think about it. He didn't need one. He's like, pretty big, you know? All I was thinking about was kind of stalling."

"You hoped someone would come? Your mother, maybe?"

"Maybe. It was just, like, two ideas. One was, quick get it over with. And the other was, put it off as long as possible, something might happen, and that was the one I was, like, working on."

"Where is your mother?"

"I don't know."

"Is it usual for her to leave you alone at night, not knowing where she is?"

"I was with my dad. She probably thought he'd stay till she got home. She's usually here when he drops me off."

Simon heard that answer and knew it was the one exception to Leni's complete honesty. She was covering for Sandra, or maybe, he felt with a jolt of guilt, exposing his own bad judgment.

"Okay, Leni. Take your time. I know this is the hard part. What happened then?"

"Right away he goes, 'Let's go upstairs,' and I go, 'Why?' He goes, 'I wanna see where you sleep,' and I go, 'Oh, really?' you know, as if I didn't believe him." She gave a little laugh then and said, "I almost said 'As if' to him but I didn't want to get him mad."

Simon saw Lopez narrow her dark eyes at that, and she spoke to Leni for the first time.

"You were trying to let him know that you knew what he wanted, sort of teasing him?"

"Well, I guess so, in a way. He had talked about hurting me and I didn't, you know, want that to happen. And I thought, like, he'll go easy on me if he knows I'm not gonna fight him, and he'll think there's no reason to hurry."

"Leni, I'm sorry, but I have to ask you this, and maybe you'd like your father to be out of the room."

Simon knew what was coming, but Leni didn't let him down. "Don't worry about it," she said. "I'm not what you call 'sexually active.'" She gave her little nervous laugh again, while everyone else breathed a sigh of relief. Simon's was the biggest.

Lieutenant Harper took over again. "But you wanted to hint to him that you had some experience?"

"Sort of. And stall and stall. So I go, 'I'm thirsty, you want something to drink?' And he goes, 'We can drink something after I see the upstairs,' you know, getting a little mad now. So I go, 'Okay, I'll take you upstairs, but first I've gotta turn out the front lights, or else when my mom gets back she'll think I'm not home yet.'"

"Clever. You were giving him something to think about. Were you going to flick the lights on and off in case someone saw?"

"I don't know what I was thinking. But he's like, 'Never mind,' and starts edging me toward the stairway."

"Had he put his hands on you at this time?"

"I was sort of keeping my distance. Neither one of us made any, like, sudden movements, and I backed up to the bottom of the stairs. Then I was sort of walking slowly sideways up. I was maybe halfway up and he was, like, on the second stair, when my dad yells, like he always used to, 'Hi, honey, I'm home,' and the ski mask goes flying out the front door, like the starter's pistol just went off."

They all smiled at that line, especially Simon who wanted to high-five his daughter for it.

They might have to testify at trial, the A.D.A. said, but probably not. Actual victims were the witnesses they needed, if the guy actually went to trial, which they doubted.

"I think Leni is a victim," Simon said, "but I hope she doesn't have to testify. Who is the guy anyway?"

"Do you need to know?"

He smiled. "No vigilantes here, Lieutenant. We'll read about it in the paper."

When they were gone, but before any delayed reactions to trauma set in, he asked, "How were you really feeling when he was in the house?"

"It was funny, Dad. I knew I was scared, but it was like I was outside the fear, you know? Something bad was gonna happen, or maybe it wasn't, but I was like looking at it happen from somewhere else."

"I'm so proud of you, honey, as proud as I've ever been."

"Even when I was captain of my soccer team and you told me how much you admired my leadership during the tournament?"

No sooner had she said this than the trembling and crying began. He had known it was coming, was glad it had come while he was still there, and he held and soothed her. He kept telling her that it would pass, that she'd feel better about it after some time, and that he'd see to it that she had help to work through it. Probably the tone and the body language got through, if not the verbal message, and she was able to go to sleep with him sitting watchfully at her bedside.

It was nearly midnight when he went downstairs and there was still no sign of Sandra. The longer he waited the more pissed off he got, but he told himself to keep a lid on it. The last thing he wanted that night was to wake Leni up with an all-too-familiar explosive scene. It wasn't the lateness of the hour that bugged him, but Leni's reluctant revelation that it had become a frequent thing for her mother to leave her alone in the house, not knowing where she was, for long hours.

Sandra walked in at about two, the little half-smile on her face a trace signal of satisfaction that she had the upper hand despite appearances, and said, as he knew she would, "What are you doing here?"

Straining to be quiet but seething with rage, he said, "The question is why weren't you here? Where were you?"

"Out," she said, the ironic smile getting a trifle broader.

"And what were you doing that was more important than being here with Leni with a rapist running loose in the neighborhood?"

"Always the drama," she said, the smile transformed into a mocking grin. "It's none of your business—or have you forgotten the terms of this trial separation? No questions asked, no explanations necessary. You can't use these random attacks as an excuse to spy on me."

"They're not random any more. He was here."

She turned serious at once, but instead of rushing upstairs to see if their little girl was all right, she gasped once, took a deep breath, and stared coldly at him. "I don't believe you."

"You'll believe me tomorrow when you hear what happened tonight, when Pete tells you or when the police or the media call you for a statement, or when Leni tells you—in case you ask her."

He started toward the door, afraid of continuing, when she said, "Wait." Those unfathomable eyes, always central to the beauty he was drawn to, were moist, and she looked at him with a calm resolve that seemed to promise rare truth-telling.

"I've been spending most evenings with Doug, and I haven't been thinking very much about anything else."

"Your gay friend at work?"

"He probably isn't gay, after all."

He wanted to ask her if she was making a man of Doug, but he held his tongue, thinking that maybe he himself was the one she was making a man of right now. And that would mean not asking the thousand questions that flashed through his mind, not grilling her and cross-examining the answers, not indulging in the self-flagellation of hearing explicit details, not making this night about him, his jealousy, and his misbegotten marriage.

She looked at him as if expecting just those things, and he felt all the conflicted emotions drain from him. His daughter had faced a monstrous trauma, and nothing mattered until that was dealt with, but his wife didn't get it. This was more than estrangement—they were worlds apart, strangers in a strained and strange misalliance. The trial was over and the verdict was in—he'd have to abandon any remaining hope of reconciliation. When he spoke, he could hear his voice reflecting her characteristic flatness and emptiness. "We'll talk tomorrow. If Leni wants to stay home from school, that's okay. Just don't leave her alone until I get here. I should be here by noon. And I'll be moving back in. You should start thinking about what arrangements you can make—and how soon."

Going South

Milt Fleischer headed to Tennessee for the 'Sixties lit with ambition and fired up with good intentions. He brought with him a New England background and three, count 'em three, Ivy League degrees. They were part of the package you got when you hired Fleischer, but he knew they could also be baggage, especially if he flaunted them, on a campus where they were rare and in a town where they, along with his Jewish upbringing, could isolate him as a stranger. "Where does an alien go to register?" he remembered his father saying as a punch line to a variety of jokes.

His high school and undergrad friends called him "Flash" for his quick and cutting wit, but he was Dr. F now, with a newly minted Ph.D. in Medieval Literature and a commitment to do whatever he could in the cause of racial justice and social progress. To his friends, The University of Tennessee seemed an unlikely choice for Milt, but the prospects suited him to a T. Comp Lit was not a department, just a cooperative program at U-T, so his appointment was in a large, diverse English Department. He'd be teaching a full load (two lower-division requirements, one upper division elective of his own design, and a required graduate course in Old and Middle English); in other words, within a traditional program, he'd have some room to flex his pedagogical imagination. He already had a record of successful publication and was sanguine about the opportunity for early advancement and tenure.

Meanwhile he was excited about the prospects for contributions to "the movement." There was no CORE chapter in Knoxville, but Milt would volunteer for a Human Relations Council that had a loose state-wide alliance. Even better, the Highlander Center, long a beacon for progressive causes but driven out of its mountain headquarters in Monteagle up near Sewanee, was temporarily housed in town while planning its new home over in Jefferson County near New Market. He hoped to bring his energy and convictions to both.

A triumph of high hopes over misgivings, Milt's first three years in the South were gratifying. In the classroom, in scholarly print, on and off the campus, in the slow but steady progress toward integration and tolerance, he felt rewarded and regarded. The crowds for an antiwar rally in Knoxville would never rival in numbers or excitement a football game or a Billy Graham appearance, but he felt comfortable with the pace of growing acceptance and in the presence of genuine congeniality among differing views—so comfortable that he could unleash Flash on occasion, like the time he wrote to the Chancellor to suggest that if there must be an Invocation before kickoffs it should be addressed to the Muses in the interest of promoting the Liberal Arts. When indeed he personally experienced culture shock, it was all the more arresting for confronting him in his classroom.

It was a class that Milt enjoyed despite having to repeat it regularly. Combining features of historical survey of English Lit (up to 1800) and "introduction to critical methods," he had developed a syllabus that arrived at a selection of Shakespeare's sonnets roughly two fifths of the way through. It was an opportunity to address three elements: Elizabethan conventions in a historical context, appreciation of the workings of formal constraints in poetry, and close readings of richly textured verse.

Perfect for these purposes was Sonnet #130, "My mistress' eyes are nothing like the sun." So there he was, in the spring of 1964, facing perhaps four or six readers with some enthusiasm, promise, or sophistication among thirty-two largely diffident, insensitive sophomores. He had already presented his simplified schema for distinguishing among the three basic sonnet structures (Petrarchan or Italian, Shakespearean or English, and Spenserian or interlocking), drawing attention to the way the "movement of material" matched the rhyme scheme itself. But he had saved presentation of Elizabethan sonneteers' convention for the discussion of this very sonnet.

Spring is a long, graceful season in East Tennessee, the redbuds and dogwoods pleasuring the senses. The class was held in one of those high-ceilinged rooms in classic-brick old Ayres Hall where the department was housed before the move to McClung Tower. It was the very room he had just left several months before when he heard the news that President Kennedy had been shot. But now, with a bright sun streaming through the tall windows at ten in the morning, all felt right in Milt's academic world.

He didn't expect that day's class to be particularly inspiring, but he would give it his best shot, beginning with what he thought was an expressive reading of the poem. Then, in his most casual Socratic fashion, Milt asked, "What do you think—or hear—is going on in this sonnet?"

Nary a hand was raised (traditional politeness and reticence being still the prevailing mode of behavior among Volunteer undergrads of that time), so he shifted ground and said, "Well, why don't we begin by looking at the form of the poem and seeing how closely the movement of material follows its rhyme scheme?"

That was the easy and obvious part, getting quickly through an assessment of how this sonnet follows the Shakespearean format. First quatrain: statement of theme; second quatrain: variation or complication of theme; third quatrain: further variation or paradoxical complication, climaxing at the end of line 12 with what seems a dilemma incapable of resolution; final couplet: almost miraculous resolution, turning the whole on its head in a clever, unexpected, thoroughly satisfying way.

"Okay, then, how are these effects achieved? Is there any variation from standard Shakespearean structure and movement? What's going on here? What is the speaker talking about?"

The broad room was built to accommodate as many as forty-eight students, although these sections were limited to thirty-two, and typically the back row of twelve was filled while the more attentive twenty were spread out among the other three rows, with only three or four sitting down front. Milt was always mildly surprised when he'd see a hand go up in the rear, and he sometimes resorted to a cheap joke like "Are you volunteering or reaching for a rebound?" But this time when a back-bencher's hand was raised he played it straight, in part because the student's face was partially obscured from Milt's view as he walked back and forth across the front of the room.

"Yes?"

"I think he's talking about a big old Nigger whore."

Some laughter greeted this remark, mostly from the back row, but even there it seemed more of a nervous or embarrassed response than appreciation of a good joke. Realizing he was being challenged, Milt walked to the center, right in front of the table that served as instructor's desk in the classroom, and recognized the volunteer speaker as Travis Sutherland. Well on his way to a lifetime as a good ol' boy, Travis was tall, sandy-haired, and blue-eyed, popular along Fraternity Row, a good athlete at the intramural level, and generally inoffensive. Milt made an instant choice to engage Travis directly in what he hoped would be an instructive dialogue.

"So, Travis, the subject of the poem is…?"

"This woman."

"It doesn't occur to you that on its primary level the poem is actually about the poet's or speaker's feelings for the woman?"

"I guess that's right."

"Then if the woman is not the subject, what is she?"

"The object?"

"Good. Now let's look at how the object is described and see how you derived your picture of her, starting with your notion that she is 'big.' Where do you get 'big'?"

The class was silent, more attentive than Milt could remember any lower-division class.

As he looked around he could see that several were shrinking uncomfortably down in their seats, while others were alertly sitting up. He felt that on the whole they were curious, maybe even excited, to see how this was going to go.

Milt waited as Travis pored over the text, evidently hoping to find a clue, and finally suggested the twelfth line where the object is described as walking on the ground, unlike a goddess.

"But, Travis, human beings walk on the ground, right? Regardless of their size? And the speaker confesses that he never saw a goddess walk, so he can't make comparisons like that. Now, wouldn't a petite woman, a creature of flesh and blood, however ample or spare, walk on the ground?"

"I guess so."

"So 'big' is your own interpretation, based on nothing in the poem."

"Okay."

"Well, let's move on to 'old.' Where do you find evidence of her advancing age?"

Again an attentive regard for the text, and then: "Well, her cheeks are pale and her breath stinks, like old and maybe sick people."

"But he doesn't say the cheeks are pale; he says that he doesn't see red and white or pink roses there. He sees real cheeks. Could he possibly be saying that this woman does not use or over-use cosmetics to render artificial decoration rather than natural appearance? And could he be implying that he prefers natural beauty to contrived masking?"

Travis was getting angry in his embarrassment, maybe even regretting his joke, Milt thought. The embattled boy said, "Didn't you tell us that every reader is entitled to his own interpretation?"

"Did you miss the second part of that? Interpretations are more or less valid depending on how the text justifies them. There is a bright line, as the lawyers say, between reading a poem and reading *into* a poem. 'How does a poem mean?' is John Ciardi's basic question for poetic interpretation. It does *not* mean, I can tell you, whatever idiosyncratic associations you choose to impose on it, that is, whatever the hell you want it to mean.

"Now, about her breath. He has perceived its odor. His olfactory organs work. But if her breath does not smell like or if it is not as delightful as some perfumes, does that mean it 'stinks'? Is it possible that almost four hundred years ago the word 'reek' might be simply a synonym for 'smell' and not exclusively for 'stink' or 'have a noxious smell'? But, granting the possibility that this woman has halitosis, is that an indicator of age? Did you ever smell the breath of a baby who has just vomited or for that matter the breath of your date under similar circumstances?"

Now Milt heard the laughter as appreciation, and he felt that he was achieving the kind of learning experience he was aiming for. He waited for quiet and then continued.

"So she is neither big nor old, so far as we can tell from the poem. Let's move on to your third characterization of her as a Negro. I won't use your offensive, vulgar term and expect never to hear it in my classroom again—unless I'm teaching certain works of Mark Twain, Joseph Conrad, or Flannery O'Connor. Where, Travis, do you find her presented as Negro?"

He was ready this time, and Milt got the impression that he had been gearing up for this. "Her breasts are not white and her hair is a growth of black wires."

"Okay. Here are some questions to consider. Can wires not come in a variety of shapes and textures, straight, knotted, coiled, wavy, or what you'd probably think of as kinked? Are there people with black hair who are not Negro? And as far as breasts are concerned, have you ever seen Caucasian skin that is actually as white as snow? Have you actually seen Caucasian breasts? Sorry, please forget that cheap shot. But you might research the so-called 'Dark Lady' whom scholars assume to have been the object of a number of Shakespeare's sonnets.

"Now finally for your label of 'whore.' I assume that the repeated use of the word 'mistress' triggers your association with prostitution, or at least a judgment of weak moral character in terms of sexual activity. But that is not the sense of the word 'mistress' as literate Elizabethans would use it nor does it account for the persistent medieval convention of 'courtly mistress' that we discussed in some detail a couple of weeks ago. By calling her his mistress the poet is couching his admiration in the conventional terms that render her worthy of the adoration bestowed on her by his poetry.

"So, Mr. Sutherland, you have taken a four-word phrase that may be indicative of your vocabulary but is surely a demonstration of your tendency to think in stereotypes and applied it, mindlessly, I would say, thoughtlessly, carelessly, though probably with the intention of getting a cheap laugh from fellow students you insult by imagining them to share your stereotypes, to a poem for which the phrase is completely inappropriate. I call that the arrogance of ignorance, but I hope it has provided an opportunity for lessons to be learned.

"Now let's all look back at the poem and read it in a different light, to learn how it attacks the current conventions of sonneteers, whether using Petrarchan, Shakespearean, or Spenserian tactics (they shared a general strategy, after all), and yet achieves the goal served by those very conventions. That is, the poet is saying how much he values his lady, so much that he refuses to use the conventional artificial terms of praise, which he calls 'false,' and yet finds her truly superior to all others. It is the power of his truthful praise, then, and his denial of the commonplace artifices by which praise is conventionally uttered, that ennobles her. Her natural beauty, unadorned by cosmetic artifice or artificial perfume, is matched and honored by a purer poetry, unadorned with cliché-ridden artifices.

"The poem, then, has as its subject and object, at its essential level, poetry itself."

The class ended with Milt's own conventional two-word coda: "Any questions?"

Milt Fleischer headed west out of Knoxville and stayed on Kingston Pike all the way to Dixie Lee Junction, where he wanted to savor a farewell taste of Ott's barbecue. And then he picked up the Interstate to begin the long drive to Seattle, after almost a decade at U-T. He had mixed feelings about leaving a place that had meant a lot to him. Ott's wasn't all he'd miss. There were the four moderate seasons at the edge of the southern mountains; the friends, students, and colleagues—though academic life dictated such passings; and the local reputation he'd earned in the classroom, on campus, and in the community.

He was proud of what he had accomplished there: meaningful experiences for students, solid dissertations and MA theses he'd directed, dozens of prestige publications including two scholarly books. He felt he deserved the senior position he'd accepted at the University of Washington. He was also pleased with the ways he'd helped move a stubborn society toward a measure of progressive adaptation. He had actually organized and led a march on City Hall to support passage of fair-housing legislation and even played a small part in the racial integration of intercollegiate sports in the Southeastern Conference.

Yet what preyed on his mind was a single egregious failure, his classroom performance around Sonnet #130 back in '64. He had reconstructed that incident in his mind a thousand times in the years since it happened, replaying it a thousand different ways. The version printed above comes closest to the way he thinks it should have gone. But in fact it had been nothing like that.

Accurate memory ends with the sentence beginning "Some laughter greeted this remark...." The rest is wistful wish-fulfillment or bitter daydreaming. When Travis Sutherland's appalling quip was uttered, Milt had been struck dumb, but less so in the proper sense of the word than in the slang. He had said nothing during a pause that seemed eons to him, perhaps also seemed longer to the class than it actually was, but was probably just long enough for a sharp intake of breath. He could never remember thinking consciously about what to do, how to handle it. It had simply never occurred to him to use the opportunity to teach a dual lesson: the one about how to read a poem and the other about racial prejudice.

Instead he taught the one and blocked the other. The reading lesson may have been pedagogically sound, even if done by rote, but to have avoided the other was to have forgotten who he was, the Flash-man of the trigger tongue and the sardonic put-down. Of course there had been many times when he'd thought of choice things to say after the opportunity had passed, the bon-mot-manqué master. Still, nothing approached the rankling regret that this scene had not been played out as fabricated above.

He ruminated obsessively about it, couldn't stop accusing himself of committing an act of moral cowardice. Sometimes he deliberately reconstructed the scene; sometimes he flashed back on it willy-nilly. He called the latter his "Flash-backs," trying to tease himself out of the shame and chagrin that it hadn't been scripted like the remodeled visions of the former. Inevitably, eventually, he would conclude that the worst of it, the part that continued to haunt him, was the instructional measure of that failure: he had never challenged Travis Sutherland for his racist joke, never discussed it with him in conference, never took it into account when giving him his C for the course.

The ultimate mortification for the instructor was that, while a classroom of sophomores had been denied a meaningful lesson that was there for the teaching, Dr. F had surely never taught Travis Sutherland a thing.

Up from Ashes, Down from Speed

They met cute. That Hollywood cliché of the early-mid twentieth century makes sense here only because it soon came to be used tongue-in-cheek instead of more appropriate descriptors like "eerie," "bizarre," "serendipitous," "beyond belief," or even "creepy." In this case, in the August gloaming on Martha's Vineyard, she was walking her sister's Airedale on the road alongside the harbor in Menemsha, and he was just coming up from the fishing wharf carrying a round aluminum container.

"Catch any?" she asked, a pleasant smile lighting up a face he saw instantly in the near dark as attractive, fair, and young--but maybe not too young for him.

"Actually I wasn't fishing," he said, then, matching her smile, "but I wouldn't mind telling you what I was doing."

"What a come-on," she said. "Go ahead and tell me."

"Well, I just scattered my mother's ashes, per her request, near her favorite waterside place in the world, Lobsterville on the Vineyard."

Her grin broadened as she approached him, the well-trained dog at her heel, and extended her hand.

"I'm Willa Sullivan," she said. "My friends call me Sully."

He reached for her hand with his right while with his left he put the canister down and extended his palm upward. The dog responded as he'd hoped she would, nuzzling his hand, then accepting his stroke of her nape as if bred to it. "Tom Davidson," he said, and stepped back to take a more careful look, taking in the slim form in the peasant dress and sandals, the reddish hair, and the broad shoulders.

"Are you an islander?" she asked.

"No, just visiting an old friend with a convenient house in Vineyard Haven. I can tell you're not a summer regular with a cottage in Chilmark, though, and not a fundamentalist from the camp in Oak Bluffs either."

"Nope," she laughed, "Just a latter-day hippie from Boulder with a sister who expects me to spend two weeks with her family wherever they're camping out each summer. It's almost worth it just to walk with Rowena here while the kids get put to bed."

"She reminds me of the Airedale of a woman I was in love with once."

"Another clever, smooth line. I bet you've used it before."

He gulped, paused, and then surprised himself by what came out of his mouth next. "Never had the chance. But truly you remind me of her, though she was dark of hair and skin. If I could see your eyes more clearly they'd be dark brown, while hers were blue. But it's the American-beauty swimmer's body that rings that old bell, brings that old belle to mind, I mean."

"Okay, you've earned yourself an audience. Tell me more."

"I'm not used to this," he said, "and I'm a little embarrassed at my boldness. But I'm just being very sentimental tonight. In fact, your coloring and open friendliness reminds me of my mother. So please take it as a goodbye and hello, not a pick-up line."

"Okay, Tom, and I think I'll start calling you Tom Terrific. Was your mother a Mets fan?"

"You're too young to remember Seaver, but no, she was a Henry Fielding fan. And how'd you come by Willa?"

Again that pleased little laugh. "Oh yeah, a Willa Cather fan. Maybe that's why I live on the border of the Middle West and try for that plain plains look."

"Nice try but there's nothing plain about the way you look."

"Anyway, what ever happened to my dark look-alike?"

"She gave up on me because I was so slow to divorce my wife before I could be sure I would get custody of the twins. But that's all right. It wouldn't have worked. We were compatible in a lot of ways, but she was a chain smoker, tooled around on a Vespa, and drank too much beer."

"We'd be all right, then," she said brightly but without being coy. And then, bringing a sudden gift of joy to Tom, "The only thing I smoke is home-grown dope and all I drink is white wine. And I can prove it."

She slid her arms around his shoulders and kissed him full on the mouth. This happened so fast that Tom couldn't believe it. But he tasted the weed and the wine and stepped back shaking his head.

Trying to regain some perspective and cover both his delight and confusion, he said, "You left out the cherry-flavored lip gloss. Can you do without that, Sully?"

"For you, Tom, that would be terrifically easy"

And so it began, right out of a when-Willa-met-Tom Saturday-Evening-Post story or maybe a b-list rom-com. They spent the next hours talking, freely and expansively, about their current lives and tastes and dreams and families, though she was reticent and dismissive about her past. There were no more kisses, but the next night she picked him up in Vineyard Haven and they drove over to the Ocean View in Oak Bluffs where the piano bar lit up what Tom called the brightest spot on the island. They picked the darkest corner of the room, though, and cuddled contentedly while the young Yale graduate played and pattered through a show-tune repertoire as if he were the loyal son of Cole Porter.

Tom was reluctant to kiss her there, where too many people knew him and no-one knew her, but after two glasses of Chablis she sought him out under the table with her hand, and as his penis rose in welcome, he said, "Do you want to get out of here?"

Half an hour later their affair began in earnest, along a quiet path on West Chop. She had come equipped--with blanket, joint, and condom, while he arrived with an eagerness borne of gratitude and frustration. Compatible to a degree of breathtakingly mutual satisfaction, they rejoiced in their startling coupling. "You are terrific, Tom," she said. "My breasts have never had it so good as with your mouth on them."

Totally overwhelmed by such post-coital openness, he rushed to gush, "You seem to know exactly what gives me the most pleasure. It's like we share a natural rhythm that can't be taught. It's heavenly."

"It's the most natural thing in the world, Tom, and I sensed from our first minutes together that we'd rejoice at being together."

Astonished at what he was hearing and feeling, he could hardly believe what he came up with next. "I can't help but think that my mother's spirit is looking out for me and blessing us."

"Maybe she led me and Rowena out to meet you. You emptied that canister and then began to fill up the emptiness in your life."

The next morning bright and early she was knocking at his friend's door. She had on another loose-fitting floral peasant dress and a wide-brimmed straw hat. The sway of her stride under the dress reminded him of the supple body underneath, and he was instantly aroused. They had walked a couple blocks toward the harbor before she spoke.

"You know I don't look far ahead, Tom, that I'm a here-and-now woman. So I've been thinking about how to spend the next three days."

"Three, but..." he began, and she interrupted.

"I'm booked on the red-eye to Denver out of Providence on Friday night, back to work in Boulder for Saturday dinner. Part-time waitressing doesn't come easy when you're on the down side of thirty."

"Well, the bad news is that we have less than three days. I have a meeting I can't miss on Friday, have to be home on Saturday, pick up the kids at camp Sunday. The good news is that the meeting is in

Providence, where I'm interviewing a guy at Brown who's the leading candidate to be our new department chairman at Maryland."

She was laughing before he finished. "Our stars are perfectly aligned," she said. "My sister lives in Barrington--that's why I fly out of Providence. Their house is comfortable and open. No pool but a great hot tub. We'd have it all to ourselves, and they'll happily stay here till Monday. Let's see how soon you can book a slot on the ferry."

Within minutes he had switched his reservation from Friday morning to the next departure at noon today, within two hours they had boarded, and within three hours after that they were naked, passing a joint back and forth, and zoning out in the eddying heat of the tub. The house was all she had promised and more. An old-brick rambler with two fireplaces, it spoke with modest claims to the comfort these people took in a design made to the taste and for the pleasure of two teen kids and their literate parents. There were books in almost every room and a sound system more prominent than the television set.

The dining room was a casual, eclectic design, but the whole effect was orderly because of the artwork on the walls, paintings and lithographs casting a peaceful aura with their rustic theme and subdued colors. And the patio with its state-of-the-art grill overlooked a yard that slanted gently down to tall hedges that assisted the towering pair of oaks in shading and secluding the advertised tub.

This is the way my honeymoon should have been, Tom thought the next day, only with hopes of many happy renewals in an open-ended future. Only here, with no promise beyond the very short term, he felt more than satisfied but not sated, as the intimacy--or "instimacy" as Willa had called it--embraced them in a vibrant state of pleasure.

Still, somewhat exhausted by the two nights of stoned amorousness, they had slept late and didn't have sex Friday morning. Willa was pouring her first glass of wine and ready for her first dip in the tub when he kissed her goodbye, saying. "I should be back by around three-thirty," and she said with a smile that could never pass as demure, "I'll leave the light on for ya."

Tom's senses seemed to be sharpened. Yes, he'd surely been mellowed out by the dreamy passage of the last few days, but instead of relaxing into some kind of thoughtless stupor he felt keenly aware of his surroundings, of the elements, and even--in a departure from his typical preoccupations with the practical details of his professional and familial demands--of himself. After a long period of deliberate celibacy, he felt that he had been released into a new phase, that he could allow himself now to open up into the possibilities of new emotional connections. That would benefit the kids, too, no doubt, since they sometimes remarked that he was overly occupied with their lives instead of living for himself. In a running joke, they kept nagging him good-naturedly that it was past time for him at least to begin having a social life. "Get out there," Doug would say, "and start dating," Jen would add, as if following a text of responsive reading. And the next day, it would be the same text, with Jen leading and Doug chanting the response.

The typically sultry midday of Rhode Island August didn't faze him. He kept his car windows open instead of turning on the a.c., breathed deeply, and prepared for the interview by reviewing what he knew about the candidate. Ralph Guthrie had seemed to be a perfect choice to succeed the laid-back gentleman who had presided over the department for a decade. High-energy was the term most often used to describe Guthrie in the letters of recommendation the committee had received.

The guy had started out as a Miltonist; his published papers, leading to a book that had re-valued *Samson Agonistes*, had established his reputation when he was barely thirty. Then he had broadened his interests, extended his prominence, pre-eminence some said, over all of Seventeenth Century poetry and on into the age of Swift and Pope. Meanwhile he was also dashing off controversial essays on the aesthetics of jazz, rock and roll, and now hip-hop and rap.

The junior members of the College Park faculty were excited at the prospect of having someone breathing twenty-first-century life into their antiquated discipline. As for the senior faculty, they were looking forward to ending the tedium of a search before the MLA meetings in December, so they wouldn't have to spend their old-home-week reunion time interviewing candidates. If Tom's on-site interview confirmed what they had already concluded, they'd gladly turn the matter over to the Dean and await the coming of their new leader.

In person, Guthrie lived up to his depiction on paper, and then some. There was an aura of energy about him that validated the hype. The way he walked down the hall to greet Tom, the firm but quick handshake, the restless stretching of his neck as he talked, these all suggested that his nervous system was charged with some inexhaustible power source. And then there was the conversation that was more like a monologue of plans, expectations, and ambitions.

When they left Guthrie's office to drive over to Federal Hill for lunch, Tom was glad to be the driver. Guthrie's knees, hands, and face were so full of jerks and tics that having him drive was to risk swerves at least and collisions all too likely. "High energy" is not the right term for this guy, he thought, he seems to be in a hyper-manic phase, and maybe it's chronic.

The Caffe Dolce Vita on De Pasquale Square, despite its pretentious name, seemed to Tim to live up to the exorbitant praise of its reviews, and if the prices were just as high Tim didn't care because he could charge it all to the department. They sat outside and Tim indulged himself with a generous antipasto and veal scallopine piccata, but he prudently declined an appropriate wine. It wasn't just the driving miles in store for him but the thought that he needed to be alert in attending to what Guthrie had to say.

There was no conversation, just a continuation of the Guthrie monologue. The man declined to share the antipasto, refused to order a drink other than iced water, and just picked at the salad he requested as his entrée. When it was time for dessert, he recommended the house special, a lavish "Coppa Syneth" Tom marveled at when he saw it at a neighbor's table. He settled for tiramisu, though, one of his standard tests for a fine Italian restaurant, while Guthrie only wanted coffee "sugar, no cream."

Watching the man at the table, more than listening to his spiel, Tom realized he was sitting with someone with such problematical behavior that he would have to be disqualified from the offer the department was about to make. It was so unnatural that Tom concluded it was the product of influence, that is, that Ralph Guthrie was a chemically dependent speed-freak. He looked for signs of cocaine or meth, registering the paradoxical dilation of the pupils in the light of midday summer sunshine.

And finally he recognized that some of what Guthrie was saying was delusional. He was talking about what he planned for the department: an agreement with the administration that they would fund several new senior positions so that he could make Maryland the Stanford of the East, a plan to establish a new scholarly journal in College Park (he had already named it "17/18" for the two centuries of its specialization), and a project for a new academic press that would be the triumph of his dynasty--and he used that word without embarrassment ("without blinking an eye" wouldn't apply, because his eyes showed constant rapid-eye movement between blinks). "I'll do for Maryland," he said, "what Matt Bruccoli did for South Carolina."

The name brought an instant image to Tom's mind's eye: Matt Bruccoli famously tooling around the S.C. campus in his bright red Mercedes. Guthrie, he thought, would one-up him in a gold-plated Ferrari zooming around Prince Georges County. The late Bruccoli, whom Tom admired for his generous appreciation of other people's work, had indeed accomplished some of Guthrie's dreams, but the results had been a mixed bag for his tenure at S.C., and besides, the times had changed to the point where the absence of a university press in College Park was an asset rather than a drain on a budget that denied urgent funding to libraries, not to mention well-earned raises to faculty.

Tom was convinced. He could not allow the Guthrie name to go forward as a candidate, and he just wanted to end this painful audition, get out to Barrington, and chill out one last time in the hot tub and Sully's warm embrace.

Chill turned out to be the appropriate word. The first sour note was the smell of tobacco he registered as soon as he walked into the house. And then the vision of sexual appetite he identified as Sully had turned into a languorous woman badly in need of a nap. The worst part of what awaited him was not only that when he kissed her he could taste the tobacco on her breath but that the cherry-flavored lip gloss had made its unwelcome return.

"How was your meeting?" she asked in a sweet but tired tone.

"Perfect--and decisive," he said. "I met with a textbook case of a speed-freak."

"That's a good thing?"

"Yes. We'll never have to deal with him again. And how was your day?"

"Okay," she said, and her smile seemed somewhat rueful to him. "An old friend stopped by and we managed to kill two bottles of sauterne."

"No wonder you look like you need a nap. Go ahead and take it. I'll treat myself to a soak and be sure to wake you in time to get a snack for supper at the airport."

She bowed gratefully and gracefully out of the room, slept a full four hours, and they were parked in the short-term lot by nine o'clock, having spoken sparely and diffidently all the way. Then, when she had checked in, she turned to him and embraced him with the full attention he had taken such delight in from their first magic moment.

"I'm so glad we found each other, Tom Terrific," she said. "But it's time to say goodbye. Go on ahead and start your long drive home. Please be careful. Stay well. And try to remember our time together as wonderful in itself as it truly was, but also that it was something to move on from into whatever here-and-now is ahead. This was loving that didn't look for more. No future, no regrets."

He bought every bit of that farewell, especially as it echoed what he had been thinking. No wonder he pondered what he registered as genuine affection and comfortable truth all the way down to the Jersey Turnpike. But by the time he cruised past the toll-booth in his EZ-Pass lane, he was already focusing on his reunion with the twins, on the anticipated enjoyment of the report he planned for the search committee, on the coming semester with new courses and new faces in the seats, and on how he might plot his re-entry, rising from the ashes, into the real but no longer frightening world of social intercourse.

The Neighborhood

Location wasn't the only reason Susan and I chose the house, but it was a major factor. Her commute to her office was cut in half, twenty minutes less each way meaning a lot to someone who worked four exhausting ten-hour days a week as an oncology nurse. Our two teenagers would have a longer way to go to school but the inconvenience was mitigated by the fact that they would now have a car to drive. Besides, it would be just a year for our daughter and two years for our son, before they were off to college.

They could put up with the smaller bedrooms, too, because part of the rationale for the move was downsizing from a five-bedroom colonial to a three-bedroom rambler. The design of the house was perfect for my needs. The lower level had a separate entrance to a space that could be divided into a waiting room and a soundproof consultation room for my therapy practice, and a large space with frpl that would serve as part family room and part studio/office.

The development was more than thirty years old, but unlike most in the area it had been built not on farmland but on wooded acres with a pair of parallel streams running through it. It had matured gracefully, and its pleasant variety of well-tended homes (ramblers, split-foyers, colonials; brick, stone, some wood-frame, very little aluminum siding; not a single McMansion) had kept the values up and the re-sales brisk.

We had a corner lot of nearly half an acre, delightful to Susan for its flowerbed and herb garden, pleasing to us both for its foliage, including lilac, azalea, and forsythia, poplar, pine, cherry, dogwood, and a Japanese cut-leaf maple that took pride of place near the front door. Not least of the attractions was the set of immediate neighbors, two of the development's founding families. On the north side were the Petersons, a pair of retired sports-minded civil servants, regulars at the community pool and tennis courts, who had raised four children in a house that featured more glass than most and who both enjoyed spending many hours on their patio or puttering around the yard.

To the west were the Whites, a retired naval officer and his wife, in a house that was nearly the twin of ours, except that it had only a little carport where we had an enclosed two-car garage. They had raised three children in that house, and though they were quiet folks who spent their days indoors, reading, listening to music, playing bridge, they were very close friends of the Petersons. Indeed, the Mullaneys, whose home we had bought, completed an inseparable sixsome who were virtually an exclusive social unit.

We had the best kind of fences that made for good neighbors, that is, no fences at all, just low shrubbery along the common borders, with breaks for easy crossings between yards, tended with care by whoever wanted to take a turn. All things considered, we felt we had made just the right move. Even financially, it was a wash. What we cleared from the timely sale of the old, larger house, covered both the new one and the careful remodeling we did to make it just right for us.

We had some concern that the Whites and Petersons would resent us for replacing their old cronies the Mullaneys, whose move to the West Coast to be near children and grandchildren might have been a more appropriate target for resentment. But no, while acknowledging that they missed the couple that had broken up that old gang of theirs, they made us feel welcome. We were maybe fifteen or twenty years younger than they, and we may still have had two children living at home, but they treated us as if we belonged, junior versions of themselves, as lucky to be their neighbors as they said they were to have us. I enjoyed playing tennis with Carl Peterson, and Susan and I both took pleasure in hearing Captain White's droll tales of the sea and the service. And the three wives communed comfortably in the yards and gardens that were their common bailiwick.

Even the fact that we were the only Jewish family in the immediate vicinity seemed to make no difference to our neighbors. In fact they had occasion to brag about the cultural, racial, and religious diversity of the community when during one Sunday brunch at the Whites' Susan joked that we had wondered if they'd say, "There goes the neighborhood," when we moved in.

Lily Peterson laughed the loudest and said, "Variety being the spice of life, you've brought us the ingredient we'd been missing."

So we had settled in very nicely, thank you. As time went by, other homes began to change hands more frequently, and always Susan was one of the first to greet newcomers. To a person, they spoke of the congeniality that seemed to pervade our streets, and our social circle expanded accordingly. As older families moved on or spouses lost mates, the mean age of our little population grew younger. There were more children around, the elementary school became crowded, and there was more lively activity in the roads on weekends. And yet the whole development seemed to maintain its traditional atmosphere and values. Election Day at the school was like a neighborhood gathering of friendly distinctions, we had our own little Fourth of July parade, Halloween brought everyone out and about (many adults in costume along with their kids), and a group of Christmas carolers made a point of keeping our house on their celebratory route.

Into this Disneyesque or Norman Rockwellian Eden some serpent of discord was bound to slither. Alas, it had to happen right next door. Susanna White's health had been gradually declining, and when the Captain had a mild stroke they bit the bullet, put the house up for sale, and moved into an assisted-living facility not too far away. The "for sale" sign hadn't been up for a week when the "sold" shingle was added—without either an open house or an "under contract" interim.

At a farewell dinner at the Petersons', Susanna assured us that we'd we pleased with our new neighbors, a scholar your age, she said, and a son just about to go away to school.

We never saw a moving van, but our friendly letter-carrier mentioned "a new kid on the block" and so Susan dutifully paid a visit of welcome with her customary offering of baked goods. She reported to me, "A nice-looking young man came and opened the door, and I could see the mezuzah on the doorjamb."

"There goes the neighborhood," I said, and she ignored the tired joke.

"He gave his name as Ari but I couldn't make out the last name, sounded something like Wolfmanjack. He was pleasant enough but clearly had no intention of inviting me in.

"There was no sign of the father. Something's not right over there, Nat."

"Learn anything else?"

"Of course. You know me. Ari is just passing through. He's making aliyah, going to stay with his sister on her kibbutz until he starts his military service, and then, he says, he'll be ready to go to college, hopes to get into Hebrew U."

Indeed, we'd see Ari walking around the neighborhood for about a week, and then he was gone. There were no sightings of his father. Weeks passed. A lawn service cut the grass, and once or twice I caught a glimpse of a tweed cap in his backyard. Susan was clearly annoyed at this reclusiveness, finally announcing her conviction that our neighbor was a spy.

"I bet he uses his children as a cover to travel overseas."

I laughed at her, arguing plausibly that there could be any number of explanations for the man's behavior. Then, one day, a substitute letter-carrier left an issue of *The Economist* in our mailbox, and I learned that one Alexander Wulfschlemmer was living next door. I strolled up the road and put it in the proper box, deciding that to introduce myself to him on such a pretext would be to invade his airspace, disrupt his chosen isolation.

But I did Google him. When Susan got home from work I could tell her that we had an eminent scholar next door. There were very few entries for him on-line, but Wulfschlemmer had done a post-doc at Harvard studying the history of ideas in medieval Judaism. In fact, Harvard had published an amplified version of his doctoral dissertation, called "Strange Associations: Kabbala and Hasidism."

"So he's poring over manuscripts, burning the midnight oil," I told her, "plying his obscure, esoteric, mystical trade."

"I don't believe it," she said. "I still think he's a spook."

As it happened, we were both wrong, very wrong. When the Petersons held their annual A.S.O. party (Autumn Seasonal Open-house, though variously mocked as "Anglo-Saxons Only" and "Anti-Social Opportunity" and "A Stupid Occasion" and "Anti-Semitic Observance"), we shared what we had learned—and suspected—with everyone there.

Most of them had given no thought to the little man who wasn't there, as far as they were concerned, but they were amused to hear of his obscure academic celebrity. The Whites were there, making a sentimental journey back home, and the Captain was surprised at what we said. "We found him to be friendly and garrulous," he said, "if a bit formal and pedantic."

Not quite two weeks later, the veil was lifted. On a Friday afternoon as I sat in the kitchen having a snack between appointments with clients, there was a gentle knock on our front door. And there stood the man of mystery, wearing a black suit, white shirt with no tie, and the tweed cap that was the only thing familiar to me about him. His full beard was neatly trimmed, and his sad dark eyes looked up at me with a reluctant gaze as I found myself surprised less by his sudden appearance than by his diminutive stature.

"I'm Alexander Wulfschlemmer, your next-door neighbor," he pronounced solemnly, but could offer no hand to shake because he was carrying a UPS carton. "This was left at my door by mistake, and I wanted to be sure it got to the right address."

"Ah," I said, "some books I ordered from A Libris. But won't you come in? We can begin to get acquainted."

He agreed, we sat in the kitchen, and he refused my offer of something to drink. Somehow it did not surprise me, perhaps as an occupational hazard of my profession, that he proceeded to tell me, a perfect stranger, more than I could possibly have wanted to know about himself. He was at his wit's end, he said, had lost everything by his inability to act.

"I'm an investor, and there have been great opportunities lately, but I sit there at my computer with my hands in my lap, unable to hit the key and make a transaction. I've missed out on whatever could have saved me. I'm ruined."

"How bad could it be?" I said. "You're sitting on a half-million-dollar property."

He moaned, then answered angrily. "You can't know how much I owe the banks. And I could have e-mailed a woman in Long Island, a widow of some means, who might have considered a marriage, but my hands were frozen—like my heart. Now everything's gone."

"Is it really too late to get back in touch with her?"

"Why would she even consider me now?" he virtually keened.

It has always been my way, in treatment, to confront a client with an obvious diagnosis. But that is something I carefully avoid outside the office, and yet I felt compelled to make an exception here.

"You're obviously deeply depressed and anxious almost to the point of panic, Alexander. Have you done anything to relieve the symptoms?"

"Too late, too late."

"Has anything like this happened before?"

He paused before nodding an admission.

"And have you gotten any help?"

"I saw a psychiatrist here a few years ago, but he did me no good, kept wanting me to take medications, which I refused to do."

This was not a discussion I wanted to pursue, not with a rigid and highly resistant man, and not when I had clients coming in shortly for my favorite kind of work, pre-marital couples counseling.

"I take it you see patients here," Dr. Wulfschlemmer said, hesitantly, and then with a touch of challenge, "Would you be willing to take me on?"

"That wouldn't be appropriate. I won't see relatives, friends, or immediate neighbors. The code guidelines aren't crystal-clear on this, but I've imposed my own standards, more practical really than ethical, and I can't begin to make exceptions now."

"Of course," he said, nodding wisely and sadly, but perhaps with some relief. He had opened up too much to me, and now he was regretting it.

"But I'd like to continue this conversation, if we might. I have an appointment due in five minutes. Let's talk tomorrow. Either I'll drop by or you come over again. We'll talk here, not officially in my office. Seriously, I'm very concerned about you."

He said no more, made a slight tip of the cap he'd never removed, and left. Wait till Susan hears this, I thought, and went downstairs to get ready for the young couple.

Next morning, as Susan went on her bi-monthly foraging expedition to Costco, I finished a late breakfast, read the paper, and did the puzzles, wondering if and when Alexander would show up. He didn't, and I decided to brave the beast in his lair. But I had barely reached my driveway when I found him coming to meet me.

"Good morning, Alexander. I was just on my way over to your house."

"Then I have saved you the trouble," he said, with a slight nod that was almost courtly.

His demeanor was somehow lighter than yesterday, but I saw that the sleeves of his dress shirt were rolled up to the elbows, and there were signs of fresh bleeding on both arms and wrists. "Alexander," I said, making no attempt to keep the alarm out of my voice, "have you been trying to hurt yourself?"

"It is a traditional way of expressing grief or mourning," he said, as if proud of himself.

"It's also a sign of suicidal thinking. I've seen it before, and I always take steps to see that the person gets treated on an emergency basis. The one thing that is constant in these episodes is that they are acute. But they're also transient; they always pass. Are there any friends you could call for help? I haven't noticed any visitors since you've lived here, but what about your old neighborhood?"

"I have never been a social gad-about."

"Any family other than your children in Israel?"

"I have two older sons but we are not close. Estranged, you might say."

"Then I must insist that you get to a hospital where you can be examined and treated right away. Let me walk you back home."

I never touched him, but felt as if I were carrying his dead weight as I guided him to his front door. His expression was impassive, and he neither assented to nor rejected my suggestion that he get a few things together while we figured out where to go and I would take him there unless he preferred an ambulance. Just then Susan arrived home, and I told Alexander I'd be right back as soon as I let Susan know what was going on.

When I had delivered my report, Susan said, "Are you sure you want to get involved? He creeps me out."

"I have to."

"Of course we do," she said. "Help me unpack the frozen stuff at least and then we'll get him seen to."

By the time we got to the Wulfschlemmer door, we had decided where to go with him—not the nearest community hospital but one a little farther away where there was a psych ward we both had reason to respect. Alexander didn't respond to the bell or our firm knocks, and, exchanging a look that said we might find a body inside, we opened the unlocked door and went in, calling his name.

What shocked us was not our worst fear but a virtually deserted, unfurnished living room and an odor that reminded us both, we agreed later, of the homes of disabled or terminally ill people we had delivered meals to as Thanksgiving or Christmas Day volunteers. We walked down the hall toward the master bedroom and found Alexander sitting at a small table in front of his computer, the screen blank for shabbat.

What followed was a wrestling match or a *pas de trois* of annoyance, aggravation, anguish, frustration, and anger. It took us five hours to get him into his car. It was always two-on-one, our insistence versus his recalcitrance, though at times we tag-teamed him and at times we ganged up as tough-cop/gentle-cop. I can't recount all that was done and said in those hours, all our arguments for getting treatment for him and all his arguments to avoid that, but some of the exchanges are indelibly etched in memory.

"I can't drive to the hospital because it's shabbat."

"You don't have to drive. I'll drive you in your car, Susan will follow in ours, and when you're ready—after sundown—you can drive yourself home."

"I can't allow myself to be admitted to a hospital because I have no clean clothes."

"Where's your laundry? I'll wash a load for you and then we can go." This satisfied him, but I thought more as a delaying tactic, because in fact Susan went ahead and took his clothes through a washing/drying cycle at our house. Perhaps the most compelling exchange was the following:

Susan: We've got to get you over there, Alexander. Otherwise we're afraid that the next time we come over here it will be when the police come to find your body.

He: Your fears are of no concern to me.

Me: They may, however, be of concern to the authorities who will support an involuntary commitment if it comes to that. The operant phrase is "threat to self or others."

He: I am no threat and you are not responsible for me.

Susan: It's our idea of a mitzvah, okay? Now let's go. This has gone on much too long, and I'm ready to call Emergency Services.

And so we went. Sat quietly in a waiting room for an hour, did his paper work because he wouldn't fill out written forms on shabbat, escorted him back to the treatment area, and waited until he was in the hands of a physician. There was no doubt in our minds that he would be admitted to the psych unit as a suicide risk. And so we could get on with our evening, which included a dinner date with old friends, though we'd have to hurry to keep our reservation.

Three hours later, as we sat watching our rented movie, there came a tapping at our door. Susan looked out the window and said, with more disgust than dismay, "It's him. Don't invite him in—or don't even answer."

I opened the door and he said quickly, "I do not mean to interrupt, but I thought I should tell you that I am back home. I could not stay there." And he turned and stepped briskly away.

"I don't want anything more to do with that man," Susan said. "Let someone else find the body."

"Well, we're not Chinese, after all. If we save his life that doesn't mean we're adopting him for the duration."

More than two weeks passed without a glimpse of the man. But when I answered the phone one morning, his distinctively flat voice with its formal enunciation announced, "I am in the hospital now. It got bad again and I knew this time where to go. Could you stop by here when you have a chance?"

I said I'd be there that afternoon and when I was allowed onto the locked psych ward was glad to find an old colleague on staff. She said she knew I'd be coming and that Alexander was doing all right, though he continued to be recalcitrant or non-compliant about taking medications. He was sitting alone at a table in the dayroom and did not acknowledge me until I had sat down. Then he handed me a key and asked me to pick up his mail, go into his house, and bring him a few things he needed—he had a short list, with directions to where I might find them (unnecessary, given the paucity of options).

I did as he asked, though it was Susan who delivered the items to the hospital without actually seeing that patient. Meanwhile I kept collecting his meager mail and checking in with my colleague on his ward, gratified that Alexander was being subjected to a course of electro-shock therapy that was apparently proving effective for him.

We undertook other measures on his behalf, though really doing it for ourselves. I called the psychiatrist he had seen and heard about a history of depression and a stubborn disregard for treatment and bitter disrespect for anyone who prescribed it. Would he see him again? Absolutely not, especially since there remained an unpaid balance on his account. And we also located his older sons, not too hard since there were only two Wulfschlemmers in all of Rockland County, New York, where we learned Alexander had left them. They thanked us for our concern and said they would drive down to "check things out."

Early the next Sunday afternoon, a black Escalade pulled into the driveway next door, and a few minutes later Avram and Yossi Wulfschlemmer were at our door, introducing themselves, thanking us again for our concern, and accepting our invitation to come in. Two good-looking men in their early thirties, they were dressed in traditional Orthodox clothing, but seemed very comfortable in it and, for that matter, in their own skin—a striking contrast to their father. Comfort showed in everything about them, their dark suits being well-tailored and their shoes noticeably establishing their affluence. Among the facts of their lives they shared with us in the next hour and a half was their partnership in a photographic equipment company with a large wholesale, retail, on-line, and mail-order clientele.

They did not seem particularly concerned about their father's condition, and though we asked no questions about that they soon let us know why. Alexander had always been given to depressive episodes and histrionic displays of anxiety. When their mother died of breast cancer just two years after Ari was born, their father had literally thrown up his hands in despair and pronounced himself incapable of raising four children. He had abandoned them to the care of the tightly knit Orthodox community in Nyack where they had lived their whole lives.

"So losing his wife triggered his first major depressive episode," I asked, the therapist looking for a quick and somehow exculpatory explanation for the behavior.

"Oh, no," Yossi said, exchanging a complicit smile with his brother. "He'd always been like that."

"Our Mom was the only parent we knew," Avram added, "and that's what made her loss so hard. As far as he was concerned there was nothing different. Instead of spending all his time pursuing his scholarly preoccupations in some library in the City, he simply moved back to Cambridge, while we mourned and were taken in by neighbors."

"He never even visited," Yossi said, "though we'd get an occasional note in the mail. He always seemed to know where we were. No wonder our sister Shoshanna grew up knowing she couldn't bear to live in the same hemisphere with him and at sixteen emigrated to Israel. Now Ari has joined her. But our life is here, a good one, too, with seven children between us and an eighth on the way. Their grandfather has never seen any of them, never even asked for a picture."

"But you're going to see him today," Susan said. "I hope you have pictures to show him."

"We're going," Avram said, without apparent bitterness, "but not for old times' sake or to rekindle family feelings."

Yossi matter-of-factly explained, "We have to be sure about some practical matters, for example, that we are in no way responsible for his medical bills."

"Or any other debts," Avram interjected.

"And we want to have access to his deed to the house, safety deposit boxes, will, and all financial records, in the event of his death. Retroactive child support is something we had long ago decided to pursue, but we haven't thought about it for years."

"Until your call," Avram added, with a kindly nod to us.

We did not see them again, nor did they tell us about their reunion visit to the hospital. Susan had invited them to have supper with us, but they declined, saying they needed to drive back home that night. The Escalade did not make another appearance.

Discharged after three weeks, Alexander returned home, but hardly as what we could call "a new man." He was outside more often, walking, raking leaves, watering the sod laid over the patch where he'd had a tree removed in his front yard. Yet there was no interaction with us, no acknowledgment of our presence, no thanks for our assistance.

A handwritten note addressed to me, left in our mailbox, was Alexander's version of thanks. It instructed me to put his key in an envelope and leave it in his mailbox. And he said, "I will thank you to stop meddling in my affairs."

Susan said, "No good deed goes unpunished, I guess. As if saving that man's life was a good deed."

But the Alexander sightings soon ceased. He had gone underground again, only to reappear one afternoon six weeks after Groundhog Day as Susan was in our garage draining the gas from the snow-blower before putting it away until next year. He came raging at her, ranting at her about the infernal racket. I heard the angry shouting and hurried out to find her staring, open-mouthed, uncharacteristically struck dumb at the verbal assault and with a look of sheer loathing if not fright on her face.

"Step away from her," I said. He did, but made no move to leave. I came close enough to him to smell the old rancid odor of his house on the threadbare black suit, and said, in what I thought was a calm, cold, and commanding voice, "Stay away from my wife. If you approach her again, in any way, I will have you committed." I told

Susan later that I should have asked if he needed another course of shock treatments, but she said that I had said enough.

I think he believed that I would and could do what I'd threatened. He scuttled away, and again for months he failed to disrupt the serenity of the neighborhood. We were, however, visited by another shock. The Petersons, who we had thought would be next door for the rest of their lives, suddenly announced that they were moving to a retirement community in North Carolina.

The shock and disappointment were allayed, however, when they told us not to worry that they were selling to another Wulfschlemmer. Indeed, they made sure to introduce us to the impressive and charming young couple who had bought the house. Bill and Kitty Costello were both lawyers, he for a large financial firm downtown and she working from home as a consultant for ecology-related outfits. Best of all, especially for Susan who missed the presence of young children in the immediate vicinity, they had a bright, polite little pre-schooler and expected his baby sister shortly after they were to move in. We quickly asked to have the right of first refusal for any of their babysitting needs. They were delighted by that and happy to continue the shared care of our bordering shrubbery.

They had been warned about our other shared next-door neighbor, but their response was a shrug of indifference. Within weeks of moving in, they seemed quite amused that a Jersey wall appeared along their border with Alexander—probably in reaction to the installation of children's playground equipment in their yard and its implicit triggering of his noise alarm. He was probably wise to do so, because play-dates became plentiful and boisterous in that well-equipped yard, with spirited sounds that I could tolerate and Susan actually relished. A couple of years went by before, they claimed, they actually saw their neighbor in the flesh. Meanwhile, little Mickey began kindergarten and we were honored to have him stay with us when his parents went to the hospital for the blessed event of Marjorie's birth.

But all of this, all that I've reported so far, is just context and back-story. The event that makes this a story worth telling, following the dictum that a corner must be turned or at least a hair to justify narrative, happened early in the Costellos' third summer next door. And it changed everything.

They had designed a thorough renovation of their yard, with a new deck and larger, remodeled patio. The first step was to rip up the existing patio the Petersons had enjoyed for so long and where they'd entertained much of the neighborhood over time. We were duly warned about the impending jackhammer assault, which we surely would take in stride and endure without offense.

After the first day's work on the project, Kitty knocked on our door.

"I think we've had our first Alexander sighting," she said, apparently trying to calm down after accepting Susan's offer of a glass of wine.

"This is news," I said as if amused, but Susan was going to take it seriously. "What happened?" she asked.

"Well, I'm not sure it was him," Kitty said, having a high regard for rules of evidence. "But Mickey described the man that came around to the house and started asking questions of the workmen. They pretty much ignored him, not out of rudeness, but they have very little English and probably couldn't understand him. Luckily—or maybe unluckily—Mickey was there and just told him, 'We're getting a whole new deck and patio.' And he left." She went on to describe, second-hand, the person Mickey had seen.

"That's our Alexander," I said. "Your son is very observant."

"Thanks. But is he safe?"

"Not to worry. The man can be annoying but he's harmless. Just tell the kids and the crew to ignore him and he'll go away."

She went home relieved and reassured, while Susan failed to accept my dismissal of Alexander's behavior as of no concern.

"Maybe he's working up to another round of shock treatments," I said.

"I just don't want him bothering those children," she said. "Please try to be aware of what's going on. If you see him coming round again, at least go out there yourself."

Two days later, the final day of intensive noise in the backyard, Susan was home on one of her rare midweek days off, and there was no Costello at home. I had just gone downstairs to catch up on some work after lunch when I heard Susan's anxious call from upstairs. "Nat, get out there. Alexander is going after the workers."

As soon as I opened the sliding door to our backyard I could hear the man screaming. The workers didn't know what to do, though they tried to tell him they were just doing their jobs. Alexander stood there, waving his arms around as if wailing about a suicide bombing and yelling words in a hodgepodge of languages, all unintelligible, an angry fit of speaking in tongues.

I got up close to him and said, "Back off, Alexander, and go home. This work will be over soon and the noise will cease."

He seemed unaware of my presence, never mind what I was saying, and continued his wildly gesticulating rant. Susan came out, took a quick look at what was happening, and hurried back inside. I knew what she was going to do, but I continued my efforts to make our neighbor understand that no one was trying to harm him, that he could go about his business and expect this noise pollution to dissipate soon. But I was speaking calm reason to a madman, and I began to be concerned that he would turn on me, spouting his venom at his old chosen meddling enemy, and I might have to try to restrain him physically.

His eyes never focused on me. I could see them wandering erratically around the scene without any particular focus whatsoever. And then, where I had seen saliva spraying from his mouth, I saw his lips begin literally to be coated with foam. My mounting anxiety was eased very briefly when I flashed on an image of Al Jolson in "The Jazz Singer," but it was only a few minutes before the emergency truck and two squad cars pulled up.

Susan's call had drawn an immediate response, our County services justifying our high property tax rate.

I never learned just what Susan had said when she called 9-1-1, but I could tell that these officers took in the scene as quickly as they needed, just as they took seriously their mission to serve and protect. Alexander did not resist them physically, but continued his manic shouting as they took him away, seating him unfettered in the back of a squad car, leaving one officer to ask us a few questions for their report. In my mind's eye I had envisioned men in little white suits fitting him into a straitjacket, instead of the uniformed men and one woman who accomplished their mission of removing an annoyance or quieting a disturbance as if it were mundane routine. We've never seen Alexander again. We don't know what happened to him, and we haven't tried to find out.

The season is turning now. It's still a little too early for the mums, but our cut-leaf maple is already taking on its rich and deeply gratifying hues. The Obama signs are sprouting in yards like the asters in the showy gardens of some of our neighbors. But our corner is unusually quiet, the empty house next door seeming to extend a somber shadow across our lawns, muting our exuberant optimism, dispiriting our complacent and warm self-regard, inverting our embrace of ecumenical inclusiveness. We are turning inward, and I fear that the neighborhood will never be the same again.

Elevator

(Homage to Robert Coover)

Car #1

Y ou could tell as they got on at their floor that they had been crying and arguing, but when they spoke their voices were composed and clear, taut and tart.

"What did you expect? You always knew I was a writer."

"And everything you experienced was grist for your mill."

"Occupational hazard."

"Your occupation, my hazard."

"Listen, if I liked what you said, and I often did, I made note of it. I used it."

"I suppose I took pride in that part of it."

"Well, then?"

"Everybody is fair game for you."

"Yes, that's the way the game is played."

"There have to be limits. This time you went over the line."

"But how?"

"That I was you in your story of me."

That stopped him cold. The door opened onto the lobby. As they hustled off, you could just barely hear their final exchange.

"Let me call you a cab."

"No, don't. I'm not a cab. And I'm walking."

Car #2

With four cars on either side of the hall, the odds were seven to
one that she would get on the one he was riding down among the
heavy traffic of the lunchtime crowd. It happened roughly once every
two weeks, but he never could calculate whether that was statistical
confirmation or statistical anomaly. The cars had no memory, he
kept reminding himself, so each time presented the same one-in-
eight chance, but the regular repetitions would seem to predict some
successes over time.

When it happened, he was always ready. And so was she, though
it was part of their routine that she would act at first as if surprised—
and then take on an air of nonchalant acceptance. Others among
the twelve or fourteen passengers might be taken aback and even
begin to express shock or outrage, but she would be blasé, ignoring
the whole thing while somehow suggesting that she appreciated it as
something she deserved, was used to, took as natural tribute to her
crowning glory.

It was all about her hair, her cascading mane of burnt gold,
uniform in its glowing color, from roots to ends, though the light
played tricks of glistening highlights depending on the angle of vision
and on the rich variety of contacts and framed glasses, some even
sunshades, of the other passengers. She wore it long, its gentle wave
flowing thickly but always without tangles or knots all the way to
her waist. Above all it was clean, and if it did not give away whatever
cleanser or conditioner she used by a palpable aroma, it was radiant in
a way that suggested whatever pleasant scent the observer—or stealthy
sniffer—imagined. Her hair was beautiful but it was an image of
health rather than of beauty that it projected.

He would always have situated himself at the back but near the corner of the car, and she would stand, eyes forward and head slightly down, as near the front center as the traffic would allow. The door would barely have closed for the descent to the next stop, when he would reach out, his arm snaking over and around anyone between them, leaning his shoulder without awkwardness toward her. It would have looked at first like the kind of gesture offered a casual but familiar acquaintance, as if he wanted to tap her on the shoulder to say hello. What a coincidence that we're on the same elevator! We've got to stop meeting like this, ha ha!

Instead, he reached out and touched that hair. She would give a slight startle response, hardly perceptible unless someone was watching closely. But the initial reach of his hand would have drawn the attention of most of the other passengers, so that her response would have registered on them. Then she would relax, with a small sigh of resignation, and she would remain still all the way to the lobby.

At first his hand would rest on the tresses near her neck, just lightly touching with his fingers stretched and spread. Then he would gently grab and hold a handful, turning his hand back toward himself as if to feast his eyes on what he had found, that wondrous hair held and beheld.

And then he would begin stroking, always gently, but smoothly, sensually, from head to waist. No matter how many times the car stopped at other landings or how many others crowded aboard, they both held their positions and the stroking went on, the smooth, gentle, sensuous caress. It was almost as if he were singing that sappy old love song with the lyric, "Counting your hair on my fingers."

At the lobby, when the door opened, the usual outward crush was augmented by a collective wish to rush from the scene of this inappropriate outrage, this violation, this transgression. It was as if there was a feeling of guilt that had to be escaped.

She left the car without haste, deliberately, while her fellow passengers hurried around and past her, none making eye contact, none watching as she crossed the lobby to wait just outside the revolving door. He too was deliberate, always last to leave the car, smiling now as the dreamy look faded from his face, the slightly parted lips curling up to show his teeth. Was that the look of a hungry man where before one might have seen a kind of wistful wool-gathering?

He walked toward her, straight through the door, and they were both smiling broadly now. The dialogue was always the same.

"What do you want to eat?"

"I don't care. Sushi? Deli? You pick."

Off they would walk, comfortable with each other and in their own skin—and hair for that matter, not touching, not a sign of intensity to dispel the image of casual companionship. They were friends, and they had the kind of private, secret indulgences that cement lasting friendships. To display the personal code in public, when the opportunity arose, made it that much more gratifying, though it would never occur to them to think about how others perceived them.

And what of the others? Most had watched the scene with a fascination they might later try to analyze, while others had looked away with embarrassment or shame at having had a glimpse of an unaccountable intimacy they would avoid remembering and never mention. A few had seen it all before. These chosen ones would routinely suppress a laugh, because, if given voice, it might have sounded more nervous than knowing.

Car #3

The elevator to the Humanities Tower was always crowded at that hour, 12:15, when the eleven o'clock classes had broken and faculty and graduate students were going back to offices or bullpens before gathering for lunch, when other staff were waiting to come down, and when some eager or ambitious or favor-currying undergrads were trying to catch a few private words with a teacher.

Jason had waited at the parking garage level, timing it perfectly so that he could be alone on the elevator before the first part of the crowd pushed in from the plaza level where the classroom building adjoined the Tower. Wearing his usual hiking boots, jeans with the hand-crafted leather belt, and plaid flannel shirt, his long, clean, dirty-brown hair gathered in a neat ponytail, he slouched against the rear wall and waited for the crush when the door opened. There were a dozen other passengers, and when the doors closed and the ambient noise of the plaza receded to a hum of quiet conversation in the car, he said, "I see you are looking at my feet."

"Oh, I know that one, Jason," said the little coed in the front corner, stooped over from the weight of her backpack, her long dark hair plaited in Native American style, smiling beneath her granny glasses, on her way to a conference with her Honors advisor. "Salinger. 'Perfect Day for Bananafish.' On his way to his hotel room in his bathrobe to put a bullet in his head. I used to wish he'd shot that loser wife instead."

"Used to?" asked the grammarian from the Classics department.

"Yeah, until I realized there'd be no Glass family saga if Seymour hadn't shot himself."

"Hey! Who fahred thet shot?" Jason was right on cue, Alabama accent and all.

"If a fart falls in the forest, and there's no one to smell it…," said the philosopher, to a rumbled reception of laughter. "Coover's 'Elevator,' right? Obvious and predictable, like what follows the chili at Bernie's Bar-B-Q, eh?"

He got off on five, and as soon as the door closed behind him, Jason said, "Strap on your safety belt, everyone! We're going to make a loop-the-loop!"

The laughing stopped, and there was a moment of silence, broken by the French professor, dressed as always as if heading for an opening at a trendy gallery, his face blazing as if he'd stopped for martinis on the way to class. "Cheever, of course. 'Christmas Is a Sad Season for the Poor.'"

One of the English T.A.'s spoke up, taking a shot at clever repartee. "Cheever to Coover, in how many moves?"

"Sorry, Charlie," said the senior modernist who had published a monograph on Nabokov, "but it's interdicted to play word golf with names of different lengths."

Charlie hung his head, but his mentor, the bright young Americanist in the department, who didn't mind fighting pale fire with pale fire, spoke up. "That's just if you play by John Shade's rules. Why not be devilish Kinbote's advocate and permit diphthongs and vowels to be interchangeable and consonants with consonant clusters, too?"

"But only once for each," said the economics historian. "It's a zero-sum game."

Jason sensed the play was getting out of his control, and he moved quickly to regain momentum. "Coover to Cheever in ten," he said, just as the car stopped on the eighth floor to let the historians out. "Coover Hoover Hooter Booter Boater Beater Beaker Peaker Peeker Peever Cheever," he called out to them as the historian left, uncharacteristically not looking back. Jason looked around at the seven others remaining in the car, shrugged in dismissive apology, and said, "Best I could do off the top of my head." Then, abruptly shifting gears, he said, "But what's that I feel on my head? Could it be blood dripping from the top of the car?"

Charlie, the English T.A., sharply, saving face: "'Silence of the Lambs.'"

"And will there be a Santa Claus cap on the body in the corner?"

The T.A. again, feeling better about himself: "A great Bruce Willis trick in 'Die Hard.'"

"And will someone get it right between the eyes when we stop at the next floor?"

"'Prizzi's Honor.'" Charlie was on a roll.

Loraine Alsace broke the sequence, her throaty voice showing off the seductive quality she'd been using on her German students for a quarter century, the felt brim of her gray hat pulled down over the darkly made-up eyes. She looked up at him sideways, a practiced, ironic smile curling her carefully painted lips. "Are you an elevator man, J.B., who makes a woman go round and round?"

"No," he said, hair-trigger quick, but acknowledging her allusion with an appreciative nod, "but I've been to Lenoir City." The T.A. looked breathlessly bewildered.

Jason whistled a dozen bars of "Miss Otis Regrets" but no one caught it, and Professor Alsace sidled out of the car on ten and away in what might have been called a slither, a slink, or a sashay.

"Picture this," Jason said to the remaining cohort of English Department and American Studies types. "A private little lift comes down into an opulent parlor with tropical décor, the grand entrance of a diva."

"Hah! I've been waiting for that one," scoffed the middle-aged modern-drama guy, dressed very much like Jason, except for the running shoes instead of hiking boots, his salt-and-pepper hair neatly coiffed over a neatly trimmed beard. "Katherine Hepburn. Tennessee Williams. 'Summer and Smoke.'"

"Gawd," said the eighteenth-century specialist, trained to out-scoff the scoffer of any century, his hair and beard as unkempt as his colleague's were neat. "Hepburn doing Williams is like Goldie Hawn as Antigone."

"Overstatement, as usual, Mason. More like Tallulah doing Medea as an Agnes Scott drop-out."

"That's cruel," said the Honors student, but she was laughing. She made eye contact with Jason and said, "It's the image of a goddess descending among mortals."

The car cleared out on fifteen, leaving Jason alone to get off at the top level. The penthouse floor was the best feature of the Tower. It was divided between seminar rooms on one side and a lounge, equipped with vending and coffee machines on the other. From the picture windows you could look down on the main quad of the old campus to the west, and from the south side you had a clear vista past the football stadium all the way to the river. On a clear day you could even see the mountains off in the distance.

Jason stood at the window for a couple of minutes, though it was not clear whether he was looking out to contemplate the scene or looking within. Then he sat in one of the easy chairs between the sofas, where he had a direct view of the elevator doors. He took a legal-size pad from his green baize book bag and began to write. He wrote "TV??" and underlined it, then began a list.

"The fall or shove into the shaft on 'L.A. Law.'

"The elevator quadrille on 'Ally McBeal.'

"And why does 'Law and Order' end so often with a tag line as the elevator door closes?"

Then he made a separate heading, "Missed opportunities." And under it he wrote,

"All those movies with the glass elevators going thrillingly up and down the modern skyscrapers and the luxury hotels.

"The open-wall elevators in lofts and factory warehouses."

He turned the page. People who got off the elevator could see him writing furiously but paid no attention. Jason at work—or pleasure— was a familiar sight in the building. Had they given it a thought or had they seen him in action in the last half hour, they might have made a number of conjectures. Was he starting to design a study on the use of elevator imagery in fiction and film? Was he going to propose an elevator passenger experiment that he and a social psychologist friend might carry out? Was he beginning to sketch out a short story for the writing workshop he was taking? Who knew? With Jason it was hard to tell what quest was next or who might be fleeced.

Car #4

He waited at the top floor until there was no one else waiting for the elevator or getting off. He stepped quickly inside and as soon as the door closed pressed the emergency stop button, knowing that the audible alarm was not working. Then he took the mirror, by the frame he had carefully adjusted, and hooked it on the handrail, near the back right corner of the car. It was angled so that with his back to the door he could see anyone waiting outside when the door opened, but in its far corner it was not likely to catch the eye of people looking in.

He was dressed in a plain black T-shirt fairly tight across his back, tucked into beltless black jeans riding unfashionably high on his hips, and black Reeboks. He was not quite skin-headed, but his hair was cropped very short with no sideburns and relatively low neckline. He had decided against wearing a cap, whether frontward or backward, though either the White Sox or the Raiders in black and silver had certain advantages. He could have been as young as sixteen or even fifteen, or as old as twenty-seven or -eight.

He took a stance facing the back wall, his head very slightly turned toward his mirror, feet spread shoulder wide, and he swiveled awkwardly around to release the stop button. He then clenched his hands in front of him, flexing the muscles of his back, stiffening his neck and shoulders, clenching his teeth to accentuate his jawline, and waited for the descent.

At the first stop, a man took one step toward the car, pivoted on his right heel in a military left turn and marched briskly toward the panel to buzz for another car. For an instant the black-clad youth thought of himself as a warrior, but in quotation marks for irony, while the brief grin of satisfaction that flashed across his face referred primarily to the ironically soldier-like movement of the coward who wouldn't dare ride with him.

A fortyish woman waited at the next stop, all got up in fur scarf and maroon hat. She stood stock still, appraising the scene inside the car, looking the passenger over from head to toe and up again, blankly taking it all in, neither blinking nor flinching as she stood there until the doors closed in front of her. Delighted, he himself stood without a twitch, but when the doors closed he change his pose, deciding that there was too little menace implied in the hidden hands.

He raised his arms shoulder-high, locking the elbows and flexing all the upper muscle groups while keeping his hands relaxed. This was a yoga pose he thought he had seen in a book, an autumn tree or something like that, which he thought might suggest great strength in repose, to be feared only if aroused.

Two elderly ladies, chatting, or as he thought of it, twittering, started into the car at the next stop. "…and then, wouldn't you know, she just…"

She broke off the story with a kind of chirping gasp, one foot inside, when she saw him, stopping her advance as abruptly as her sentence. Her companion bumped into her, followed her gaze, and quickly retreated. Both ladies had turned tail and were scampering on little bird-steps, as he thought of them, almost on tiptoes, fleeing down the corridor in search of safety. He gave himself a mental high-five and flexed for the next stop.

"We'll wait for the next car," the young matron said, holding two children by the hand, firmly preventing them from entering what she seemed to be characterizing as an overcrowded elevator. He thought he could glimpse some other people waiting behind her, but no one made a move to get on. He was decidedly pleased, almost giddily triumphant.

At the next stop, just four stories up from the lobby, two boys, nine years old by his estimate, plunged promptly into his space.

"Watcha doin', mister?" said the first.

"Nothing," he said, dropping his arms.

"Exercise, maybe? A little tai chi?" said the other, but talking across him to his friend rather than up at him.

"Nah," said the first. "Not in jeans."

He turned around now, and the boys looked frankly at his face.

"You sure you're all right?" asked the second boy.

"Yeah," he muttered.

"Leave him alone," said the first, but the second wouldn't let it go.

"Some kind of game?" he said, and, with no answer forthcoming, added, without the slightest hint of judgment in the observation, "That you play with yourself?"

The car stopped and the doors opened onto the lobby. The boys hurried out, but the second one looked back over his shoulder and said, "Don't forget your mirror."

Indeed, he had forgotten it. He took it now from its perch on the railing and was looking directly into it when the doors closed and the car began its rise back toward the top.

Car #5

At the ground floor, a little girl stepped primly from the car, followed by her mother. She was four, her curly hair in natural ringlets to her shoulder framing a smiling, pretty, green-eyed face. If Bill Robinson had been there, they could have danced and sung "Good Ship Lollipop."

The mother turned back and held the elevator door open, because another four-year-old stood in the corner, dark hair in bangs and sparkling dark eyes highlighting a biting smile and a look of grim determination. The girls were twins, looking nothing alike, dressed in becoming individuality except for the matching pairs of velcroed sneakers with flashing colored lights. Not identical, their parents always said, but sororal twins.

"Come on, Julie," her mother said evenly, with just a trace of impatience. "We need to do our errands."

"No. I want to stay here, Mommy," the child said, clearly and without petulance, though she reached up now to grasp the railing with both hands in an attitude of determined recalcitrance. These were children who had breezed past any terrible twos but were entering a stage of two-squared with a multiplied sense of insistence. They insisted on their own styles, colors, tastes, and autonomy. Decisions were not to be passed along and accepted or even participated in; they were to be asserted, and if thwarted these girls would stand up for their entitled choices. Besides, how could you know what you wanted until you knew what your sister didn't want?

A man approached the car as if to get on, and the girl outside said, "My sister doesn't want to get off." He had already turned toward the other express car and pressed the button before she had finished.

"Julie, we have to go. Now!" Her voice and pitch were raised in emphasis, but if there was a tone of annoyance it was eclipsed by a sense that the very act of raising the voice was unwanted and unwonted in this mother.

"Why can't I just stay here?"

Resigned, but determined to be in control, the mother reasoned with her. "Julie, you know that we can't leave you alone. Besides, you and Molly have an appointment with the photographer, and we're meeting Daddy there, and he's taking us to lunch."

Molly was really enjoying this. It was her turn to be the good sister, and she wished with all her good heart for Julie to carry on with her bad sister act. When two women approached the car, she smiled at them, waved a hand toward the scene within, and pointed them toward the other elevator doors. She couldn't help grinning when she heard her sister say, "I'm not hungry, and I'm tired of taking pictures, Mommy."

Knowing they were approaching a standoff, Mommy shifted into diplomacy/deception mode. "Look, honey. Your choice is between going with us, having a good time with your family, and getting all our errands done before we come back for some games and maybe a video this afternoon—either that, or you can stay right here in the elevator. But you'll be stuck in it, riding up and down by yourself, all day, because it has a locking device that won't open the doors when a child is in it alone, not until a parent comes."

Julie considered this carefully. These express elevators were very fast, so fast that every time you rode in it, up or down, your stomach jumped. She didn't like the feeling of her stomach jumping, but what she did like was the waiting for it to happen, trying to guess just when it would, and the feeling of having done something dangerous after it happened. It was exciting before and then a thrill. She didn't know it, but she was doing a classic risk/reward assessment.

She was just wondering what it might be like to do it in the dark, when her mother probably reading the looks that crossed her face, surprised her, reaching in and taking a firm hold of her shoulder. She lost her grip on the railing and found herself being propelled through the elevator doors. Molly was waiting, took her sister's welcoming hand, and they skipped in step toward the street entrance across the shiny marbled floor of the big lobby, leaving the many smiles of bystanders and passers-by in their wake.

Their mother took no particular delight in the little battle she had won in the ongoing war of her twin-raising. But the pleasant picture of her girls in front of her gave her more joy than any thrill of victory she'd ever known, a kind of express elevator for her mood. She looked forward to telling Tim about it, not at lunch, though, not in front of the girls. It wasn't dining-out material anyway. She'd save it and savor it, telling him tonight, maybe after they were in bed, but not before she'd made the entry in her journal about it.

Loose Ties

Megan and Rachel had a lot in common, their friendship of five years a natural result of their proximity and the main conditions of their lives. Both were divorced mothers in their early-to-mid-thirties, whose cheating ex-husbands had left them with two children to care for while working to keep the homes that were part of their settlements.

Theirs was a friendship of convenience. Megan's kids were old enough to babysit for Rachel's, so that at least once a week they would get together at some sidewalk café for a glass of wine or two, chilling out for an hour or so, talking about nothing in particular, laughing about the cartoonish flaws of their exes, and sharing the craving of two ex-smokers. They never discussed anything to do with religion or politics, having polar opposite views, but occasionally trading glimpses of movies or TV shows they had often dozed through.

Their main topic was the men in and out of their lives, comic exchanges about the slim pickings out there for women in their shared situation, though their contrasting social styles made these anecdotes mutually amusing. Megan was a nurse in a family practice office where she had opportunities to flirt with many a dad who appeared regularly. With her China-doll features, bright green laughing Irish eyes, and quick tongue, she triggered many a passing shot, sometimes accepting an invitation for a drink or a meal, but always with practiced discretion.

Once in a while she would allow herself more than the harmless repast, especially if the dad was equally discrete, reasonably attractive, and--especially--generous. She also had a knack for transforming such brief encounters into friendships, so that she seemed always to have men around, men who could provide professional services without charge or help her when she needed work done in the house. She liked having men around. She listened to what they had to say. Except for her hours with Rachel, she always had a strong hand pouring her wine--and covering the tab.

Rachel, equally attractive with her dark hair and eyes, a flair for funky apparel, and engagingly forward conversation, was flirtation-averse. In the large company where she worked as a mid-level Jill-of-all-trades, she had several friends among the largely all-male staff. They were men who never made a pass, treated her as one of the guys, and never had to bite their tongues on four-letter words around her. Any "asshole" who did come on to her in the office, single or married, was summarily sentenced to a perma-freeze shoulder.

Still, she was interested enough in men to have ventured into the jungle of on-line dating services. Her own profile was rare for its total honesty, while the men who responded were typically accomplished liars, socially inept, or phony Narcissists--and often married. She was lightning-quick to judge them, rarely even completed an evening with them, and never took them home. The only "match" she saw a second time was a man her age but more than twice her weight; he told her that her athleticism inspired him to get back in shape, but when they had a second dinner together he began promising to lavish her with luxuries if they could become a couple. She left her share of the check (unlike Megan, she always went Dutch) and walked out.

Telling Megan about her dating misadventures, Rachel realized that while her friend may have been listening her attention was always past her shoulders. Wherever they were, Megan was scouting the talent, checking out the men who were paying attention to them, sometimes catching their eyes or even face-flirting, as she called it.

Rachel was having none of it, and so they developed their private joking routine about the "bar scene." Rachel told tales of men because she had none. Megan rarely mentioned her men; they seemed more like extras than courters in her scenario, as Rachel saw it. Neither envied the other, nor was there any trace of pity. One way or another, men were jokes between them, and they enjoyed the humor that bound them together.

All that began to change, at first gradually, when Megan began to see Larry. A new patient at her practice, Larry had caught her attention with his quick tongue and sly persistence. Pushing fifty but looking forty at most, he too was divorced, the custodial parent of two children, but he was just a couple years out of a long marriage and the two daughters were away at school. They had lunch, they had dinner, and just like that they were in an actual affair. He was filling her calendar, and on those weekends when her boys were with their dad he stayed over in her bed.

She saw Rachel less and less. The old routine, where she'd drop the boys at Rachel's house in Kensington and they'd go into Chevy Chase for a wine-break, or Rachel would bring her kids over to Bethesda and the two moms would tool down Wisconsin Avenue to a DC watering hole, became a rarity. And when they did get together, the roles were reversed. It was Rachel who listened, without passing judgment, to Megan's complaints about Larry.

"I think he's crazy," she would say. "After we have sex, he'll spend an hour telling me stories of his life."

"Is he trying to impress you?"

"Why would he? He's already in my bed."

Six weeks or so into the affair, on Christmas day as it happened, Rachel knocked on Megan's door, knowing that the boys were with their dad and Larry had stayed over. "She was just being nosy," Megan told Larry later. Much later, Rachel told Larry that she had just wanted to see this "old Jewish professor" she had heard so much about.

As for Larry, he often told anyone who'd listen that as soon as he saw Rachel the thought flashed in his head, "I'm with the wrong one."

It had been one of those rare December warm spells in Maryland with temperatures in the sixties, and Rachel had come straight from the tennis courts, dressed in white shorts and a funky t-shirt top. Sedentary Megan smiled patiently as Rachel and Larry began talking about their running and their tennis, politely and casually suggesting that they might get together to hit or run together. Otherwise, they all seemed to hit it off well, and Rachel was soon included in some of the social plans Megan and Larry were making. All this while Megan complained to Rachel about Larry's quirks and Rachel held her tongue and passed no judgment.

When a Willie Nelson concert at the Capital Centre was announced, Larry got four tickets. He had arranged for a shy young accountant who was a regular in his poker game to be the fourth. Teddy was reluctant to be Rachel's official date but as a Willie fan himself he went along for the ride. Rachel didn't care. She loved Willie too and had her heart set on a night out, with the added bonus of Larry's promise to score a joint or two for the occasion. Teddy and Megan were weed-avoidant, so the great pleasure of the evening for Rachel and Larry was to pass a joint back and forth in appropriate appreciation of the Willie Nelson experience.

Rachel maintained forever after that she didn't take this growing nearness personally. But Larry claimed that the whole evening was part of his Machiavellian plan to woo Rachel—or at least to open a crack in the door of her distant heart. In any event, other cracks were becoming evident. While Larry never got past the stage of semi-cordial distance with Megan's boys, he was beginning to show an affectionate interest in Rachel's kids. After a run or a tennis match with her, he might hang around to give little Lisa a bike-riding lesson or Nate a chess lesson.

He had also begun to worry about Megan's devotion to the fruit-of-the-vine consumption, asking Rachel if she thought there might be a problem. And while he began to grumble to her about Megan's exes showing up at the Bethesda house at all hours, Megan was bitching that he was hanging around so much he seemed to take her for granted. Rachel had no response to either complaint, until a major crack in their little social firmament occurred in mid-spring.

Larry was away for a long weekend, helping a daughter move, and Megan filled her own dance card, first, with one of her exes and then, curiously, with a blind date from out of town. Larry made a rare display of anger, though he tried to pass it off as bewilderment.

"Why would you do that?" he said.

"Why not? I'm entitled to have fun, not just when you're around."

"I thought we were being exclusive," he said.

"But we had no such understanding. At least I had never heard anything of the kind from you."

"So much for understanding the natural development of close ties."

"Closed, you mean?"

"And you thought you were closeted?"

"Well, then, I'm free, white, and single, and now I'm out of the closet."

Rachel heard this conversion repeated by both her friends, verbatim, and this time she had a response. "If you meant to send him a message," she said to Megan, he probably got it. If you didn't, what were you thinking?" To Larry, she said, "That's just what she would do, and she's not going to change for you."

The next time Larry stayed over at Megan's was the last time. Over his orange juice and her coffee, they smiled easily at each other with an exchange of glances that all but said, "That's that. It was good while it lasted."

"What's it been," he finally said, "about five months of intimacy?"

"Yeah, and I hope you appreciate what you've been given. But it's not going anywhere, right, and so you'll be moving on."

"And you'll stay right where you are."

"This might sound funny to you, Larry, but I'd really like it if we could stay friends, even if we never share a night in bed again."

He didn't laugh, but it crossed his mind that she'd probably had this same conversation half a dozen times before, and that some of her exes did in fact continue to see her from time to time. Sharing a bed? Who knew, but so what?

The pause was brief, but he said, "Sure," not sure that he really meant it. "So it's not going to bother you that I plan on seeing other women, probably starting next weekend."

Her smile was as warm as ever, and she said, "Not at all. But promise me one thing, that you'll stay away from Rachel."

He'd been thinking more and more about Rachel and wondered whether Megan had finally figured out where his affections might be redirected. She may not have been prescient, he thought, but she wasn't stupid. In any case, although he was affronted by this request, he wasn't going to deny that Rachel would be his primary target in weeks to come.

"What? What gives you the right to attach conditions to our presumptive friendship, not to mention yours with her? Suppose Rachel thinks it would be okay to see what might develop between us?"

"I just don't think I could take it. In the first place, I don't believe it could possibly be anything but another short-term fling for you. No way it could last."

"Well, don't worry about it. If it happens, it happens--and you'll be the first to know, I'm sure."

With that, he made a quick retreat, realizing he'd actually been giving it more thought than he'd ever let on to Megan. He also realized that Rachel would not take kindly any sudden change in their second-hand connection. They were already close friends, but to sense a sudden shift of his affection from her friend to her own self would be a losing proposition, so to speak. His age notwithstanding, Larry thought he could take his time, and besides there were a couple other women he thought he might pursue in what he was already thinking of as a transition period.

So he made some dates--with the grad student mathematician he had been admiring on campus and with the special-ed teacher who had audited one of his courses and seemed to be flirting with him after class. He was still seeing Rachel fairly often, running, playing tennis, and having an occasional meal with her kids; and he was careful to hint at the social calendar he was filling elsewhere. Rachel had shrugged off the break-up with Megan, and the two women had resumed their occasional evening of wine-tasting, once with him even volunteering the babysitting duties.

But as time went by, the spring dwindling down, and finding that other women interested him less and less, he decided he could no longer afford to play the waiting game. He had felt close enough to Rachel to tease her about her on-line approaches to match-making and persuaded her to show him a draft of the new introductory letter about herself she was preparing to post. This was a deliberate ploy. He was planning a direct line of approach. He practically memorized her letter, focusing on the surprisingly frank details she had spelled out in her self-profile. And that night he wrote a letter in response, an honestly complimentary tribute but more important a remarkably complementary (if somewhat creative) sketch of himself as a perfect match for her.

Next day he invited Rachel and the kids out to his house and cooked dinner for them. They all praised the taste of the hamburgers that he grilled after showing them the way he kneaded horse radish into the patties. And as the kids settled down in the mellow after-meal to watch a video, he presented the letter to her. She began to laugh right away as she read it, but was actually blushing by the time she had finished. And that's when he asked her out "on a real date" for that weekend, dinner and a movie.

"Sorry," she said, "I have other plans."

Larry didn't hide his disappointment. He had put too much faith in the winning wit of his strategy, and then she smiled warmly at his long face and said, "I have a better idea. I've been offered a pair of tickets for the Orioles game on Saturday afternoon. Would you like to go with me?"

"Game on," he thought, then said it aloud.

They drove up early, found a good parking space near Memorial Stadium, smoked a joint in the car, found their seats in the third row behind the third-base dugout, had dinner in Little Italy, and drove home singing old pop songs together. Did he spend the night? No. Did he even kiss her goodnight? No. He made a move and she dodged. No matter. They were on their way, both tacitly agreeing to let the courting begin.

There was no whirlwind to it, just a steady crescendo of closeness throughout the year and well into the next. Larry had told her what Megan had said in their last morning's conversation, and Rachel laughed it off. But they were so busy with each other on a daily basis that they hardly noticed that Megan had been out of touch.

One day in Georgetown, walking up Wisconsin Avenue after a business lunch with a group of her co-workers, Rachel spotted the China-doll face of her old friend walking toward them. She quickened her pace toward her, expecting to greet her with a hug as of old, when Megan saw her coming. Instead of consummating the chance reunion, what Megan did was stop short, cover her face with her hands, and turn away into the gutter.

That night, when Rachel told Larry about it, he shrugged it off and said, "She'll get over it. After all, she already knows that this is no short-term fling." Rachel looked doubtful but nodded her acceptance of that generous prediction. And it wasn't more than a few weeks later that she was calling her sister on Long Island and saying, "He mentioned the m-word." She did not, however, share the same news with Megan.

They were heading steadily toward second marriages. Larry had even asked her children for her hand. "Cool," said Nate. To Lisa,

Larry said, "What would you say about me becoming your step-father?" "Okay," she said, then adding the literal-minded twist that often livened her conversations, "but then you'd have to marry my step-mother." Larry found in Rachel's parents a congeniality that he'd never had with his ex's family, and when friends of his wondered about his taking on the burdens of surviving two more adolescences, said, "I'm looking forward to it--this time with a collaborating partner."

So they made their idiosyncratic plans. They would have the honeymoon first (Jamaica, toward the end of winter while the kids spent an almost-spring break with their father), then the wedding party the night before the ceremony in May (they called it "a New Era's Eve party"), and a morning service with just intimate families in a rabbi's study. They shared so much together, including aspects of their first marriages, that their coupling was almost too easy. They were a match not only in cultural heritage but in shared tastes in books and movies. Not only were they physically compatible but they matched strides in their runs and played close tennis matches. She even matched his enjoyment and knowledge of spectator sports.

They were blessed beyond words and yet canny enough to count their blessings. On the honeymoon, during one sunset watch in Negril, Larry said to Rachel. "Wouldn't you like to have Megan come to our wedding party and hear us toast her for her role in bringing us together?"

"Of course."

"Then let's send her a picture of us here at Pete's and tell her we owe it all to her and would she please be the first to accept an invitation to our party." And so, dear reader, he wrote it.

Megan ignored it.

"Maybe," Larry suggested to Rachel not long after the nuptials, "her idea was to challenge us, a little reverse psychology to make us prove that it was no passing fancy between us."

"You mean like 'The Fantasticks,' the two sets of parents arranging their children's marriage by building a wall between their homes and forbidding any interaction?"

"Right, a reworking of the old Edmond Rostand play, itself an inversion, like Romeo and Juliet, of the story Ovid tells about Pyramus and Thisbe." Larry had learned to hold his proclivity for pedantry on a tight leash, but sometimes it just ran away with him.

"The what? Never mind." Rachel had learned to ignore these outbursts but on rare occasions she reacted verbally, with or without a rolling of the eyes. Quickly, she recovered and said, "No, Megan could never be that subtle."

In years to come, on celebrations of their tenth and twenty-fifth anniversaries among many other occasions, they would joke with each other about whether Megan might be ready yet to acknowledge that it was no short-term fling after all. And whenever anyone asked about how they met, they always heard a consistent version of this story.

There would come a time when Larry could tell a simpler version of "how I married your grandmother" to Lisa's children. That tale even came with a fable-like moral: "There are ties that bind but others that unwind. Some losers can't keep them tied or abide those winners who can and do."

They Were the Fiedlers

I must have been three or four years old when I first became aware of the Fiedlers. I was thought of as a shy and withdrawn child, but in fact I was a reading prodigy much more involved in the world I encountered between the covers of books than with the world outside--including my parents' social life. My brother Ben knew the truth; he was guiding, and enjoying, my early education.

It was hard not to notice that a group of four couples gathered at our apartment for an evening of bridge every four weeks, and at first the Fiedlers were just two of the crowd, along with the Lessers and the Zellers. We were the Millers and still are. Entranced by words and names, I realized that all our names ended in "-er," and I imagined that this connection had formed the group. Later on I would sense some even more mystical or magical force at work when I became privy to the origins of what I called the Tuesday Night Bridge Club and learned to recognize distinctions among the members.

At five, for example, I knew that Golda was Bill Lesser's wife, that Paula was Stan Zeller's, and that Louise was Bill Fiedler's, though to me they remained for many years Mr. and Mrs. I believed that there was some magical element in the duplication of names in the group; besides the two Bills, my mother shared the name Golda with Mrs. Lesser.

When my father came to New Haven to start a business as a wholesale appliance distributor, his necessary first connections included a lawyer and an accountant. Lesser and Zeller were highly recommended, and they both found Max Miller to be so congenial that they quickly included their wives in social occasions. The Fiedlers soon followed because, coincidentally, Bill Lesser and Stan Zeller were also Bill Fiedler's lawyer and accountant. In the mid-'30s, with the recovery from the Depression barely underway, these were folks communally striving to achieve middle-class independence.

It took me some time to learn what Bill Fiedler might have done for a living--and I was never actually certain I knew. I had heard him referred to as a furrier, but also gathered that he had interests in various rental properties. One property he owned outright was a farm in Wallingford, where his widowed mother lived and where acres of cash crops were rented out.

The bridge game rotated among the four couples, and they all seemed to enjoy their Tuesday evenings together. They played for modest stakes with the losers paying into a fund kept by Stan Zeller. At first once, then later twice a year, that money covered the costs of vacations that they took as a group, while their respective children stayed home with supervision from an assortment of grandparents, aunts, and uncles. There were eight of us, including my brother and me, one Lesser son, a Ziegler brother and sister, and three Fiedler kids.

Starting when I was seven, there began a tradition of the four families gathering on weekends at the Fiedler farm in Wallingford. Once or twice each spring and fall we were thrown together, a motley crew with no cohesion that seemed to matter other than that our parents enjoyed playing cards together. My brother was the oldest of the progeny, and within two or three gatherings after he turned fifteen he found reasons to be otherwise occupied on those Sundays. The next oldest was Max Fiedler, who thrived as the leader, especially when some athletic competition was involved--softball or touch football. His sister Clara was always an eager player, and it was immediately clear to me that these siblings had a close connection played out in

Clara's eager athleticism and Max's enthusiastic appreciation of her charming presence.

The magic, it seemed to me, was still at work in the duplication of names. The first-born Fiedler son shared his first name with my father Max; the Lesser son shared his with Stan Zeller; the Fiedlers and Zellers had daughters named Clara; and the Millers and Zellers had first-born sons named Ben. All these repetitions had been bestowed long before the Bridge Club was born. Only Beth Fiedler and I (the matchless Noah) had unduplicated names among us all, and at some later time that struck me somehow as part of the magic.

Ben Zeller was Clara Fiedler's age, but she pretty much ignored him, with his reluctance to perform athletically. Still, perhaps because of his stoic acceptance of being the last player chosen for any game, she made sure that the rest of us welcomed his participation. Chronologically I came next but felt no close connection, especially in my brother Ben's absence. I enjoyed the games, but mainly amused myself by watching the interaction of the other kids. Clara Zeller, with her long golden hair, was gracefully un-athletic, seemingly floating above the activity and smiling down on it all. Shy young Stan Lesser, I thought, had a puppy crush on Clara Zeller; he seemed to regard her from near and far with dogged appreciation, while she never took notice of him. The youngest was Beth Fiedler, pretty, somewhat dramatic, and appreciative of the pet-like attention that drew everyone to her.

We all had to earn our game-time by working around the farm, picking corn, tomatoes, berries, or grapes, with only Clara Fiedler seeming to enjoy it. In bad weather we played a variety of games indoors, and I found it interesting to see that there was little change from the way we interacted in the fields: Max Fiedler the leader, his sister Clara his devoted and gregarious sidekick, Beth the charming mascot, Clara Zeller the aloof beauty, her brother Ben the grudging participant, and Stan Lesser a brooding outsider. Our parents let us do our own things, though Louise sometimes poked her head in and distributed her warm smiles around the whole scene.

On those bridge Tuesdays, what drew my attention, once I took an interest in the action and distinguished among the bridge players, was the byplay. Bill Fiedler was the life of the party, robust, red-faced, overweight, joke-cracking, and raucously appreciative of the jokes of others. Mr. Zeller and Mr. Lesser were the quiet ones but glad to play straight-men to the comedians, while my dad was second banana without seeking star billing. Max Miller must have had some inkling of the magic of names, I thought, because he had called his business "Max Sales Corporation" with what I believed was a punning cleverness. It was his name, after all, but the phrasing suggested he hoped for maximum business.

He was the best card-player in the group, though my mother was just as sound a player if a less adventurous bidder. Without prejudice, I understood early on that bridge was just an excuse for getting together, and that my parents, who were pretty serious about the game, played under wraps on club nights while reserving competitive (and sometimes incendiary) play with other couples they came to know in town.

The women were gentle and warm, each attractive in her own way. Paula Zeller was always carefully made up and neatly dressed, her hair still blonde, and her demeanor carefully attentive. Golda Lesser was more casual and quieter, but there was an appealing sweetness about her that made others warm to her. Of my mother's red-haired beauty and graciousness I was well aware, but it was Louise Fiedler that I singled out for particular attention. Dark-haired, petite though not as fashionably slim as Paula, brown-eyed, and both in appearance and manner a thoroughly embracing woman.

I'll never forget the night when she announced to the group, within my nine-year-old hearing (though no one there knew how much I always tried to hear their banter), that she was pregnant. There was general hooting and hollering, an uproar of surprise and teasing in which they all took part, while a glowing Louise and a gloating Bill seemed to bask in the attention. Apparently no one noticed that I had stuck my head into the room, checking out the rare boisterous behavior. In retrospect, what finally registered on my amused but somewhat bewildered naiveté was that the whole communal atmosphere in the club would change with the birth of this surprise event.

The changes came gradually, but within a year there were no more Tuesday-night bridge games. Joel, another name with no echo, was a sickly baby, and Louise became preoccupied with his health. If her other children were unhappy with her new focus, not to mention her significant absence from their customary full-family involvement, they never showed it. In fact, they all made a big thing out of their much younger sibling, doting on him and devotedly entertaining him. It reminded me of the way my brother Ben looked after me, especially when I was sick enough to stay home from school.

The Lessers virtually disappeared from the social life of the group, though Joel's arrival could hardly have been the cause. Bill suddenly gave up the practice of law, his clientele having dwindled with his interest, I think now. He had invested in a personal-service company, primarily a laundry with home pick-up and delivery, and that came to occupy most of his workday hours. Golda became withdrawn, almost agoraphobic, while Stan, benefitting from the new source of income, was sent off to private school and later boarding school.

If the parents' bridge game no longer bound the families, another factor worked to maintain the ties. Louise had a cousin in New York who ran a boys' camp in summers up in the foothills of the Berkshires. Max Fiedler, Ben Zeller, and I, starting from the summer I was eight, were regulars. Max starred on the camp's baseball team, a center fielder with a gift for racing to the spots where balls were hit and then stand waiting for them. The phrase "Fiedler the fielder" tickled me; there was a magic at work in the playfulness of anagrams.

Eventually the camp turned coed, so Clara and Beth joined the small New Haven contingent. Clara Zeller did not; in fact her brother Ben had already faded from the group. During one of my junior high school summers, Clara Fiedler took it upon her graceful shoulders to teach me, a socially immature boy, to dance. I loved her like a big sister, while failing to appreciate the way her little sister was maturing into a pre-teen beauty.

Speaking of little sisters, my oldest grandson called me on my birthday last summer and said, "Happy birthday, Grandpa. You may have noticed that, now that you're 85, you match my date of birth- -8/5/85--and that means that you were born in '31 and now I'm 31."

"Thanks," I said, "I used to think about the magic of numbers. Maybe that's inherited--and skips a generation. But I'd never forget that your sister was born on 9/2/92." That call delighted me, triggering a powerful memory for this story. Back in the day, our telephone numbers had only five digits. Ours was 61850, the Fiedlers' 81506. That confirmed a magical connection between us, I believed. At that time I was known at school as Know-It-All Noah, with a precocious numeracy matching my college-level literacy. What were the odds that the same five numbers would be interchangeable in our small area (never mind that I could recall them today). Without putting pencil to paper, I calculated it as better than 833 to 1, surely a sign of a mystical connection.

The warmth I felt for the Fiedlers was hardly cooled by tragedy. Joel, always a sickly child, succumbed to leukemia, then virtually untreatable, before he had even started school. The Fiedlers took it hard, and my mother and I, alone of the old crowd, grieved with them. Max seemed relatively untouched; as a high school senior he had become a champion junior tennis player. In fact, he was favored to win the state title. But the night before the finals he went out and got roaring drunk and could barely see the ball during the ugly match. His drinking, in secret for a couple months, as I see now, was his escape from his little brother's death and his family's grief.

Life went on for the Fiedlers. They regained their old habitual welcoming warmth, though my parents had become socially distant.

Not so I. I would take the Whalley Avenue trolley and transfer to the Whitney Avenue bus several times a week to be with them. The rest of the original group lived on the west side of town; I could have walked either to the Zellers' house on trendy Colony Road or the Lessers' two-story clapboard on Sherman Avenue. The Fiedlers lived on the approach to East Rock, on Orange Street.

Max was away at college and Clara starting junior college as a commuter from home when their dad had his fatal heart attack. The shock drew a large crowd of old friends around them, but what impressed me most amidst the outpouring of community sympathy, was the steadiness with which Louise held herself and the surviving family together. Her daughters reflected her strengths.

Through junior high and high school, their house was like a second home to me. Clara was ever cheerful, supportive, and funny. Her nickname "Cocky" advertised her status as life of the party and center of attention. She had many suitors but never coupled with anyone--until Albert came along. I admired him, thought she deserved him, an exceptionally bright and personable doctoral student in psychology at Yale, and I liked the attentiveness he paid to her. I was the first outside the immediate family to know when they became engaged and the only one in my family invited to their small wedding.

The Wallingford farm was gone, to support Ben through law school and help him establish his practice, I supposed, and to pay for Clara's modest wedding. My first year away at college, my most faithful correspondents were the Fiedler sisters. Clara addressed me as "Brother, dear" and signed off "Love, Sis," except for the one letter that hailed me as "Boy Wonder" for having made dean's list without the effort of opening any books. She chided me for not fulfilling my promise and ability. While I seemed to take pride in my schoolboy nickname of Know-It-All, she alone had realized that to me it was a hurtful put-down. She knew I took pleasure in my mental precocity but also that I resented being isolated because of it. So now she cheered me on, acknowledging my powers and urging me to put them to use and erase any stigma. This time she signed off with "Love, Cocky."

Beth's notes, full of teen angst, the frustration of sometimes not getting the best parts in plays, and requests for help with English assignments, also closed with "love," but it felt perfunctory to me and not supported by the tone of the text. The last summer before she went off to Emerson to pursue her dream of a career on the stage, everything changed. Clara was gone: Albert, not a clinician but a researcher, had earned a post-doc at NIH and they had moved to Bethesda. That ample three-story clapboard at 729 Orange St., always a house of warmth and mirth for me, had fallen into disrepair. It was under contract for sale, to make way for a McMansion I supposed and to cover Beth's tuition and Louise's relocation.

What grabbed my attention, though, was that Beth's beauty had blossomed. and I lusted after her. Rumor had it that she enjoyed "putting out," that she was happy to "go all the way." Perhaps this should have cooled my ardor but seemed instead to arouse my fantasy that we were destined to be a couple. The timing itself was magical when by the end of July she had broken up with her high school boyfriend at the same time that an intimate relationship of my own had fallen apart. Beth and I spent many August afternoons and most evenings together, growing ever closer--but not physically. Our hours-long conversations were intense, as her higher education loomed alongside my impatience to get through with an unproductive and aimless baccalaureate.

We never spoke of being or even getting together during the fall semester, and we both went separate ways during breaks. Then, one late spring evening, after an exchange of phone calls, I took her to dinner in Boston, with a classmate (who had joined me on a round of interviews) and his fiancée. Beth turned in a brilliant performance. She was effervescent, attentive, affectionate, all touchy-feely. The other couple joked that we might beat them to the altar.

Later, after a goodnight kiss, she said, "You'll always be my intellectual love, Noah, but you'll never be my lover." This sounded to me like a rehearsed curtain-line ending the long dialogue of our evening, if not the charged tension of the last summer. It also disappointed me, though I resisted the urge to applaud.

That was the last time I ever saw Beth Fiedler, which was neither planned nor deliberate. Our respective plans, schedules, and developments took us on ever-divergent paths. I saw Louise, however, whenever I visited New Haven or even passed through, though those occasions grew fewer and farther between. She was there in the crowded reception at my mother's funeral. Two years later she was the only one of the old crowd at my father's. I had actually fantasized once or twice during those two sad years that there would be a Fiedler-Miller coupling. All our subsequent meetings, however, were at the care-home on Ocean Drive in West Haven, where she had a view of the Sound from her rocking chair on the porch. She seemed always glad to see me, happy to hear of my family and doings, and apparently never forgot from one time to the next what I had told her.

Louise never seemed to age. Her smile was strong, her hair barely gray with a lot of black left, as if she had weathered all the emotional storms she had survived. Clara and Albert had settled in Bethesda, he had risen to the chairmanship of his department, and they had two kids; but they never exchanged visits. Beth had won an internship at the Guthrie Theater after her sophomore year and never came back from the Twin Cities; she had married a professor at the university in Minneapolis, had two children--and they never visited Louise either. And at some point her son Max had died, though I can't date the event and only got a meager newspaper account.

Max Fiedler, a modestly successful attorney, single and solitary, had died in his apartment in Milford, sleeping on his sofa in front of the TV, when a fire destroyed the place. Yes, he was a smoker, and yes, he had probably never given up his appetite for liquor. So far as I could tell, there were no ambient factors to suggest suicide. I never pursued the case, nor discussed it with anyone, but to this day

believe that it was suicide. Call it a bias, but I believe that people with
live cigarettes in their hands who have had enough to drink to put
themselves to sleep have killed themselves. In my imagined scenario,
Max's depression had deepened when his sister Clara left him for a
life with Albert and he had never found anyone to fill that void--and
perhaps never tried to fulfill a meaningful life.

Years, even decades, pass and sometimes even the most divergent
paths may cross again. My final academic appointment brought me
to Bethesda, and I promptly got in touch with Clara and Albert. My
marriage was coming apart, two children (the clear standard in our
generation) unable to sustain it; but my wife and I agreed to have
dinner with these old friends, though my wife had shared nothing of
my closeness with the Fiedlers.

It was not a successful evening. My wife was her characteristic
aloof if beautiful self, disdaining to engage with these people. Albert
dominated the conversation with his narrative of his department
and its research projects. And there seemed nothing left of the old
affection between Clara and me, Cocky Sis and Boy Wonder having
grown worlds apart.

It saddened me that her old ever-present world-warming smile
never brightened the evening, even as we compared notes of our
children. My efforts at shared reminiscence were wasted. Any mention
of Max or Beth was so flatly ignored that I felt cut off from what I'd
always felt was a life-line. No warm sisterly hug. Instead of rejoicing
at our reunion I felt the grief of a mournful wake and despairingly
bereft of anyone to share it with.

Somehow, and I never learned how, after our separation had
become official, my soon-to-be-ex-wife got a clerical job in Albert's
department at NIH. And less than a year later, I learned of Clara's
death. It staggered me as the most inexplicable thing I'd ever heard.
She had died in the hospital in a self-induced diabetic coma. Another
suicide in the ideally happy family I had firmly fixed in my memory.

I was shocked. How, I wondered, could a mental health professional not take better care of a severely depressed (and diabetic) wife? I was enraged, but not primarily at Albert. Rather, in my self-absorbed anguish, I burned with questions. How could I not have known about the diabetes? How could I not have known about the major depression? And how could I not have known about the hospitalization? In other words, how could my ex, who had contact with Albert every day of the work week and regularly with me through our children, not have kept me informed? It was, I understand now, convenient to have another reason to rage against her, though even then I knew that there was nothing I could have done for Clara.

I had one final visit with Louise, a little more than two years later, when two major changes had taken place in my life. One was that I had become a regular volunteer on a suicide hotline (in part, an homage to Clara), an activity that led me to go back to school for a degree in clinical social work. The other was that there was a new woman in my life and that we were on our way to marriage. The first was something I wouldn't consider mentioning to Louise, but the second was something I wanted her to know.

Lucy and I had been to New Haven for the wedding of a good old friend's older daughter. Lucy knew that we'd be stopping in West Haven on our way home. She knew much of this history. In fact, I had told her that she reminded me in some ways of the Clara I had loved and wanted Louise to meet her. We didn't stay long, rocked on either side of her on her porch, and talked about our plans.

Louise must have been close to ninety then and had hardly changed. She calmly greeted us, said nothing of the past, had no complaints about her present life, and gave us her blessing with a warmth that evoked her better days. I didn't expect I would see her again, but assumed I would get a report of her demise, if not from Beth then from someone who knew us both. In the absence of such a report, I sometimes think that she's still looking out on the Sound, peacefully taking in the passing scene. She'd be pushing 120 now.

They were the Fiedlers and the line had ended, at least as far as the name was concerned. The bits and pieces of this chronicle, the small moments of our connection, the second-hand reports of momentous calamity, all gone. We are still the Millers, now two mature generations down the line. Yet I know that the Fiedlers are parts of who we are.

Lobby-Sitting

This story begins, as so many do, with a coincidence. I am sitting in the lobby of the convention hotel in Santa Fe, when I see walking by a man I hadn't seen in almost fifteen years. He and I had had something back then. I wouldn't call it a fling, it wasn't a one-nighter, and it never became an honest-to-god affair. I guess you could call it a connection.

We met at an event very much like this one, a regional academic-literary conference, where we both presented papers on the same panel. Mine was a leisurely fifteen-minute analysis of a short story by Eudora Welty, a lucid if rather elementary account of meaning as seen in the story's imagery and mythic allusions. His was a rushed twenty-minute presentation called "The Dance of Fiction" that looked at four quite different stories by disparate writers in a way that was so sophisticated you couldn't follow it in an oral delivery.

We were delivering these exercises primarily because in the early days of careers it was de rigueur to pile up credits for a c.v. that would satisfy requirements for tenure. And, in their quite divergent ways, these pieces were determining factors in our future. Mine was heard that day by an editor of *The Sewanee Review*, who liked it and later published it. I never thought it was that good, but over the years *Sewanee* has sold reprint rights dozens of times. Yet it was within months of its delivery, having derived neither satisfaction nor pleasure from the exercise, that I decided to leave the profession and pursue a kindlier occupation, becoming a physical therapist and practitioner of therapeutic massage.

His piece, soon published in *The Paris Review*, was the making of him, providing an overnight reputation as one of the brightest young critics in the field. Over time, that reputation, ironically, led to the career he actually coveted, as a rising administrator in higher education. His paper took a single short story each by Zadie Smith, Barry Hannah, Carson McCullers, and David Leavitt, and asserted that they were characteristic of each author's narrative strategy and verbal idiosyncrasies. He paraded the stories out for us to admire their decorative nature and then paired them off, Smith with Hannah, McCullers with Leavitt. They--the stories themselves, not the writers--performed some fancy steps, a pirouette, a jeté, and a variety of pas de deux.

I sort of got a handle on what he was doing, though it was a bit hard to follow where he heading. And then he had them change partners, Smith with Leavitt, Hannah with McCullers, and they reprised their paired high-jinks. Yet again they switched, Smith with McCullers, Hannah with Leavitt, grandly brandishing their wares as they whirled, until finally they reverted to their original pairings for a last round-up.

It's a quadrille, I finally saw, the late eighteenth-century form for four couples, before it became an eight-party party-piece. And what, I wondered, did it say about the stories or the writers? Well, nothing. It spoke only to the cleverness of the critic. No wonder the chosen passages contained no dialogue (never mind that dialogue is central to the form and to the style of these writers): this was not part of a critical conversation that enhances literary value; it was criticism as performance art. In the present context, since there's no dialogue here, if I were a post-modern critic myself, I would call this observation a bit of negative-self-reflexivity; but I'm past all that.

In the hours that followed we never spoke of our respective papers.

We talked academic trivia: the way the system worked, how to play the game, who was going where, and the like. We shared a late lunch, a bottle of Australian white, and, one thing leading to another, a king-sized bed for the night. The sex, when it came, was rather perfunctory, and I got the impression that his mind was elsewhere, maybe planning his next career move. And yet I agreed to meet him at the next regional convention in four weeks' time. He used the term "hook up" and I didn't correct his usage, where calling plans for a second date "hooking up" was a contradiction in terms.

We had agreed to meet at a publisher's party the evening after his appearance on yet another panel. Those were the headier times when such perks as free booze and examination copies of new books were still offered up to all ranks. The hookers, it was said, left town during academic meetings, while the liquor purveyors prospered.

The panel was a discussion of post-modern fiction. It was the first time I ever heard the word "pomo" uttered live by a talking head, and I realized that despite my perfect progressive profile I was afflicted by a severe case of pomophobia.

In any event, he was at the epicenter of the Harcourt party when I got there, but we were soon isolated from the room's action and interactions. We were engaged tête-à-tête, and yet I watched him looking past me to take a census of the gathering, registering names and affiliations. It was his way of working the room with his eyes, he said. He took obvious delight in committing such details to memory, almost as much as his pleased satisfaction when someone recognized him for what he had read at the last meeting, which had already appeared in print. The term "tour de force" was used, perhaps with tongue in cheek, but he practically preened to hear it.

We lingered rather longer than I would have liked, but he seemed to be in his element. I have to say that the bedroom was not his element, as I rediscovered that night, but I enjoyed other aspects of this connection. His analysis of professional peer review for articles, for example, was an ironic set-piece, demolishing the practice as an example of cronyism-on-steroids passing for honorable practice. Then he placed it in a larger context of how the good-old-boys network controls the whole academic apparatus and ethos.

The surprising thing was this: instead of leading him to turn against the profession, he took his cynical knowledge of the system as providing opportunities for him to race up through the ranks. It was administrative heights he aspired to. Students were burdens, teaching loads were to be whittled away to nothing, and research was a hindrance to enjoying the professorial life while grants weren't necessarily correlated with production. Besides, administration was where the big bucks were. He not only fantasized about chairmanships and deanships; he was planning on them--maybe with a university press directorship thrown in for lagniappe.

What drew him on was turning me off, pissing me off, too. Still, when he asked if I would be at the early-November meetings I shrugged my way into accepting the implied invitation to a third date. We met in the hotel lobby, where I took in his expertise in the art of lobby-sitting. His eyes made complete circuits of the area, and he seemed to recognize every face without any accompanying welcoming acknowledgment. If lobby-sitting were an Olympic event he'd compete for the gold medal.

When we parted next morning, it was with a sense of farewell. He was crestfallen if not disappointed that I wouldn't be at the MLA meetings between Christmas and New Year's. It was less a matter of wanting to see me than it was the loss of a kindred colleague in the game. Missing MLA was tantamount, he said, to a rejection of the profession, and incidentally a personal affront to his ambitious embrace of it. But that was what I had decided. I wouldn't go to another meat-market for intellectuals and poseurs. I was rejecting the academic life and lifestyle, and I was rejecting him as well.

I spoke of coincidence at the beginning, but I haven't identified it. It wasn't the mere fact of seeing his face again after fifteen years. After all, when I impulsively gave up an afternoon of my vacation week in Santa Fe to revisit the kind of occasion I had gladly walked away from, I knew there was a chance he would be there. This was hardly a case of walking into the one gin-joint in the world where he was. In a vague and distant way I had kept up with his progress. He'd either be recruiting promising young colleagues for the department he was now chairing or interviewing for a vacant deanship, maybe right here in New Mexico.

No, it was this: walking into the lobby I had picked up the current copy of the *New York Review of Books*, less to catch up on the world of sophisticated letters than to mask a non-member's lack of a program. Then, sitting down and unfolding the tabloid-shaped anything-but-tabloid publication, I had seen his name on the cover. Neither bold-face nor fine-print, his name was that of a kind of mid-list contributor, and I had just registered this as a fact of his life when I caught sight of his face.

He must have seen me, too, because even as he strutted purposefully through I could see him doing his working-the-big-room thing. He neither slowed down nor even blinked. He had successfully blanked me out--as I had him. Once he'd passed, I started to read the piece, his first published work as far as I knew in about a decade. Ten years before, his second article ("Narrative Formalities") had appeared in the stodgy old *American Literature*. One of my clients had brought it to me, saying, "Didn't you know this guy? Check it out."

I read it with bemusement. It began the same way as his first big hit, with a formal presentation of four short stories--by Bernard Malamud, Laurie Colwin, J.F. Powers, and Alice Munro--and the assertion of their representative quality. The difference was that the selections were introduced in a staid and formal way instead of the flamboyant showiness of the other. The word that occurred to me was "stately," which invariably triggers in my readerly mind the opening of *Ulysses*--which I then begin to parody as "Smarmy, glum Huck Finnegan," before I could control the obsessive tendency.

Once again, the figures are paired off, Malamud and Colwin,

Powers and Munro, changing partners twice before returning to
the pairing we rode in on. In this case, though, the tricky steps are
replaced by an almost robotic if still graceful processional. Okay,
I thought, I get it. It's a minuet, and you, my friend, are a one-
trick critic. And why not? Fool them once and you get tenure and
promotion; fool them again and you earn a shameful chair.

And now, breaking into the intellectual big time with the *NYRB*,
he had completed his winning trifecta in the game of showing what
really matters. He had chosen to perform a few limited exercises in
an arena where he could demonstrate that for all readable literature
what mattered was the cleverness of the reader. This time, given a
five-column spread, he had pulled together a memorable if motley
chorus line.

Prancing onto his entry stage, skipping with a sprightly
youthfulness that belied their age, were stories by Irvin Faust, Ishmael
Reed, David Foster Wallace, and Raymond Carver, squaring off
opposite selections of Cynthia Ozick, Grace Paley, Anne Beattie, and
Jayne Anne Phillips. At least he had not used any of *The New Yorker's*
underwhelming "Twenty Under Forty" to prove he was *au courant*.

"Fiction Do-Si-Do" was his title, and he pulled out all the stops,
swings, and loops of a western square dance. The cadence of the
narration was bright, perky, and explicit. You were engaged to follow
along to its beat, and I found myself mentally clapping hands with the
childlike rhythm of it. The dancers, it was clear, are like replaceable
extras in the production; the star, with billing over the title, is the
fiddler who calls the steps for all to follow.

Obsessively, I read--or lilted--through to the end. Why these
storytellers, I wondered fleetingly, and not Fitzgerald or Hemingway
or Faulkner or Roth or Updike; why not Flannery O'Connor or
Katherine Anne Porter or John Barth, Salinger or Cheever or Coover,
George Garrett or Harvey Swados or Mark Schorer, why not Bobbie
Ann Mason or Lorrie Moore or Peter Taylor, the protean Jerry
Klinkowitz or the irrepressible Lewis Nordan for that matter? Well,

of course, because any old hack could be booked; the entrepreneur could sell his gossamer wings as first-class flight. I recognized the addictive draw of the old academic games--and their self-imposed limitations. He could have had them all dancing at a gala. What a ball he could have had.

With relief, satisfaction, and an inward smile I put the thing down. I felt as I had when I finally kicked my Spider Solitaire habit cold turkey, deleting the insidious game from my computer. This story ends, as so many do, with a question: What did I ever see in him?

Sophie

S he was surprised at herself for being so excited about this party. At age 24, after all, she had been to a hundred similar affairs. And besides, it was just another in a whole series of events she had attended with Irv Friedman as her date, going back to when she was 17.

Growing up in Altoona, with a small, tight Jewish community that could barely support its one Conservative congregation, she had accepted the proposition that her choices of male companionship would be severely limited, at least until she went away to college. It was almost as if, in that community, marriages were prearranged by sets of friendly parents like traditional Indians of matching castes, by the time of the girls' confirmation when the boys were just graduating high school.

Good old Irv was actually three years ahead of her and already a freshman at Brown when he came home to escort her to her confirmation dance. Good-looking, always smartly dressed, good-natured, and easy-going, Irv was almost too good to be true, especially as he treated her with a respectful consideration that spoke of a generous devotion to her. She was led to believe, with a clear consensus around town, that she was a good match for Irv--good-looking, witty, well-mannered, and artistically talented, therefore perfect marital material for a future Jewish doctor in Altoona.

Except for one thing, that "almost" in her perception of him, a touch of effeminacy that for a couple of years at least she could easily ignore. But it was "touch", or its absence, that was a puzzlement to her. His affection for her was clear, but affectionate gestures were beyond him. Except for the considerate way he held her when they danced together, and he was the best dancer she knew, she never felt the caress of an embracing hand. Not only was she a virgin when she graduated high school but she had never even been really kissed, an embarrassment that she shared only with her kid sister. This absence was virtually enforced by the fact that whenever an escort was called for, Irv made sure to be the chosen one.

Irv would come home from Providence most weekends during her senior year and made it his business to see her in Bethlehem the next year when she was a freshman, if she hadn't gone home to Altoona as well. The following year saw some changes. Without ever discussing it with him, Sophie began to date other guys--there were Jewish boys at Lehigh who showed an interest in her. And Irv, though he had chosen Perelman for medical school, his dad's alma mater, found it difficult to keep up with his schoolwork, especially in the labs, and often failed to make the short trip home from Philly or even to Bethlehem.

So the kisses and caresses began to come Sophie's way, much to her relief and much to her pleasure as well, but second base was as far as she'd ever let a young engineer go. The boys, on the other hand, seemed to be put off by her long-term connection with Irv that was received as common knowledge in her circles. "It's a small world," she'd heard a thousand times, "especially if you're Jewish."

It had sometimes occurred to her that Irv was gay, if closeted, and perhaps intimidated to come out because of parental pressure. It was universally expected in Altoona that he would eventually join his father's OB-GYN practice--and by inference that he would marry a local girl. Guess who. Sophie simply put the whole issue out of mind, settling on the proposition that Irv was simply that rare asexual male she had read about in her psych class. Rather than consider him a long-term consort, she began to use the still frequent occasions of being Irv's date at major events to cultivate connections with his friends, particularly the old fraternity brothers from Brown who kept showing up and even showing an interest in her as a possible target of affection--or lust.

So when she had moved to Boston, with a part-time job at the art museum while she pursued an MFA degree, and Irv was doing his residency at Brigham-Women's, their history of regular dating practices was conveniently revived. Tonight's party was a regular event, held every other year at a mini-mansion in Newton, following the Brown-Harvard game. Maybe this would be the time she got lucky, not how the men used the term but in the sense that she could meet someone who would take her seriously, someone she could take seriously, that she'd find her match after all.

Instead of being disappointed, her excitement grew almost as soon as she went through the door. Suddenly she became the object of attention from two of Irv's old friends, fraternity brothers of his at Brown. She vaguely remembered them from other times but never had gotten to know them and certainly had never felt their spontaneous admiration. Suddenly the name of Sophie Weiss was heard throughout the rooms of hard-drinking, hearty celebrants of a rare Brown football win in Cambridge, She was the center of the party, being vigorously pursued by two unattached men.

Except that they were only temporarily unattached. Both had married right out of college, even as they had begun graduate school, Ben pursuing a doctorate in literature and Billy an MBA at the Harvard Business School. Roommates as undergrads, poker-playing and partying buddies, they had stayed in close touch while their paths diverged widely. Sophie took her time absorbing, or partly inferring, a thorough assessment of them, one that she felt entitled to since they were competing for her attention, Ben getting her to dance as much as he could, Billy trying to corner her with concentrated serio-comic and wide-ranging conversation.

The latter began to wear on her. Blond Billy was tall and slim but without the grace she typically associated with that body-type, and as she looked up into his broad grin she thought he bore a resemblance to Eleanor Roosevelt. He was entirely too full of himself for Sophie's taste. He let his brilliance be known to the world, as he sailed through the b-school, landed a Wall Street job as an analyst for a major brokerage, and had recently moved on and up to a hedge fund that was going to use his abilities more productively and make him rich doing it. He had already fathered three children with his earth-mother-type wife, though his reputation as a universal skirt-chaser might have produced other pregnancies along the way. His attention to Sophie was focused, but it was clear to her that it was his regular m.o.

It wasn't working with her, in any case, and she eventually allowed herself to be "rescued" into the devoted attention of her other apparently smitten pursuer. Ben was shorter, wiry, an accomplished dancer, with large sad brown eyes that seemed to hunger after her. When he ended one dance by kissing her, it didn't surprise her, but she experienced it as a serious overture. She enjoyed it with a kind of thrilled merriment, regretting it at the same time. It was what she had been wanting and missing all this time, and she hated that it had come from a married man, a match that was impossible.

Ben seemed to grasp her mixed emotions, and he greeted it with the story of his unhappy marriage, a tale she accepted as genuine and not just the cliché line of a wandering cad. At least, she thought, it wasn't that other cliché she told jokes about: I love my wife but oh you kid. Ben wanted her to know that he was drawn to her because she was everything his wife was not, funny not tragic, warmly pretty not icily beautiful, and, he added hopefully, responsive to him not provocatively repulsed by him. The bottom line was this: he didn't know why he'd been cursed by such a marriage or how, in spite of all, he'd been blessed with two beautiful children; that under no circumstances would he abandon those kids or compromise their lives with anything less than his full fatherly presence.

She answered his sad smile with one of her own, saying, "That's too bad. We'd gotten off to such a promising start. I almost thought we were a perfect fit." He was leaning in to kiss her again, but she parried the thrust with a question. "But Ben, where are your children now?"

Now he grinned, caught in the act of running away with his feelings for her. "Melinda comes from money," he said, "and that translates into frequent visits to her parents' place on Longboat Key. The kids enjoy being spoiled there and I trust my in-laws either to be a buffer keeping their daughter in line or to let her pursue her own interests--whatever they may be—while they babysat."

Sophie changed the subject. No more intimacies, she thought. And they spent almost three more hours talking about anything other than themselves, until Irv came around to take her back to her apartment. She was sorry to leave Ben's company, but she had learned that he was teaching at NYU downtown, in a tenure-track position he was lucky to have landed in a tough market. And she had given him, without embarrassment or trepidation, her address and phone number, because he seemed so eager to maintain some kind of connection with her--and she believed him, not just wanted to believe him, but believed him in a way that felt comfortable and natural to her.

Over the next six or seven months Ben validated that assessment. Every two weeks or so he'd call her or write her a letter, friendly and newsy and joking, only rarely suggesting that he'd like to see her again. Was he courting her, she sometimes wondered and then wondered why he would. Yet she felt that she wanted him to play that role. When she dated other men she always compared them to Ben and found them wanting.

And then her life as a twenty-five-year-old virgin took a dramatic turn. With her degree soon to be in hand she began applying for jobs--in New York--and making trips to the City for interviews. On the very first of these rounds she asked Ben to meet her for lunch, as she put it, "to process the process" and talk about the pros and cons, the likelihood or unlikelihood of possible offers, her impressions of the world she was about to inhabit. She made it easy for him by suggesting they meet in the Village, though she only had about an hour and a half between meetings uptown.

They embraced when they met, and she tasted the first kiss as a total reentry into the magic she'd experienced at the party, natural and exciting and right. And then they laughed and ate and talked like the friends they'd become without physical contact. Such meetings became regular as she pursued whatever possibilities opened up for her. He asked the right questions about jobs and companies, and without making suggestions led her to accepting a position as an artistic executive with a small ad agency, with offices, as it happened, in the Village. From there it was an easy shift to helping her find a walk-up studio apartment in the East Village.

This was love, Sophie thought, and to hell with his family. She was going to make him a gift of her virginity, and she thought more about hoping he'd appreciate it than about what it would be like for her. In fact, when it happened, on a glorious October afternoon, in her "loft," Ben was the nervous one, Sophie the calming, welcoming presence.

Their subsequent meetings were regular if infrequent. They'd meet for dinner, alternating between out-of-the-way Thai and Mexican places near her place, with an occasional pasta treat at Minetta's. Sometimes they met in her loft to make love first, sometimes with somewhat more haste after dinner, and sometimes not at all. What they enjoyed most was the comfort and ease of their conversations and shared humor.

The changes in the routine came gradually, troubling Sophie not at all. This is what she had settled for and she continued to feel good about it. Comfortable in her own skin was the way she put it to herself, and she began to date other men sporadically, even occasionally having casual sex (without the passion she experienced with Ben) and rationalizing that it was hardly life-affirming but not really awful.

Ben, on his part, saw no other women, and she had no reason to doubt it. He never indicated that he wanted more of her time than he was getting, and he never wavered in letting her know how much pleasure he took in her company. If he had fewer occasions to see her, there were two reasons. As his children grew, he took more and more seriously his role as the appreciative and attendant parent. And as he settled into his academic life, always marked by devotion to students and his classroom performance, he began to work harder on publishing scholarly essays and working toward his first book. She was appreciative of all of this, and as they approached the first anniversary of their affair felt a kind of security in what she had, without wondering how much longer it might last.

Shortly after getting home from work one evening, her buzzer sounded and she gave her usual "Who is it?" response.

"It's William Siegel," came the authoritative voice. "I've come to see you."

She immediately buzzed him in, an almost automatic response, though she realized later that there had not been the slightest tingle of pleasure, pride, or embarrassment in the sudden appearance of a man she hadn't seen in about two years. He filled her doorway when she let him in and lurched awkwardly to embrace her. She stepped back quickly and saw that he had gained some weight along with a self-awarded gravitas, almost laughed to register that his receding hair had some gray in the yellow and that he looked now more like Teddy than Eleanor Roosevelt.

"How did you find me?" she asked, even while realizing that she didn't care.

The answer was rapid-fire, "Well you know I have a steel-trap mind and I never forget a pretty face. I had plenty of data to work with and lots of good sources. You weren't that hard to track down."

Now Sophie began to feel uneasy, wondering why it had taken so long. Instead of the good-natured if rollicking drinker she remembered,

Billy seemed to be on some kind of manic high, maybe the effect of coke or some other kind of speed.

"Before you take off your coat," she said, "tell me this. Why me? Why now?"

And he rushed to answer. "Because of Ben, of course. I thought that since I had slept with his lovely wife, why not his lovely girlfriend?"

Sophie did one of her repertoire of nimble dance steps, ducked under one of his still outstretched arms, opened the door behind him, and silently gestured him out into the hall. He turned and stepped out through the door, obviously taken aback by the rejection, and began to mutter an incoherent rebuttal. She shut the door firmly and locked it, waiting until the man had loudly started down the stairs, before she headed for the bathroom for the quick shower she needed.

In no way had she welcomed this intrusion, and she was pleased with herself for the way she had managed her escape. The rudeness disgusted her but she assumed that the man's colossal ego would never entertain the thought of trying it out on her again. But now she faced a dilemma. Should she tell Ben, and if so how? She didn't need to tease him about other guys paying attention to her. There were some at work she'd tell him about, and he'd be more pleased than jealous. And she felt no qualms about letting Ben know what a churlish, betraying oaf his old friend had become. No, the issue was whether she needed to tell him what Billy had said about sleeping with his wife. Could it have been true or was it just a misguided come-on? If true, did Ben know? If not, did he need to know? Or what would it mean to have her be the one to tell him?

In the end she decided, with just about the same kind of determination as when she had decided to go to bed with him. It would be her second major gift to him. She would never mention it.

Change, as one of her favorite songs said, was "gonna come." The first big one was that her sister Miriam followed her not just to New York but to the East Village. Miriam was the literary one and she had landed an entry-level job with a small publisher. She was also the more outgoing party-loving one, darker and more vivacious than her sister, and if not quite as pretty more available sexually. They grew closer than ever in Miriam's first few months in the City, and Sophie's social life multiplied with the events and friends who were glad to bring them to all sorts of ad-agency and publishing parties.

Ben never met Miriam, as Sophie deliberately kept them apart, not for any pettily jealous possessiveness nor any long-buried shame or guilt. It was just that she saw so little of Ben, less and less as the months passed, that she wanted to keep their times together separate, as precious as possible, even as her feelings for him changed. She loved him but realized that she was no longer in love with him.

Yet another change occurred within their coupling. They began to collaborate on cartoons. Ben would come up with ideas and Sophie would draw them. Some of his notions came from contemporary automobile traffic situations. He came up with a series involving a family on a road trip responding to signs on the road, with the young son waving signs with answers to what road signs said, for example, "Are you kidding?" when a sign read "Are you speeding?" in a traffic jam, or to a scene of multiple signage of ads and directions: "Fewer signs = fewer accidents." She argued for "less" instead of "fewer" in that one, but he insisted on the grammar of it. Others were signs answering common bumper stickers. If a car's sign said "Baby on board" the kid would be waving one that said "Aargh! Prepare to walk the plank" with a skull-and-crossbones design.

She loved his wit; he loved her art. Her favorites were ideas drawn from classical or biblical sources, like the one showing a voluptuous Delilah lazing on a sheepskin-covered couch, while a hirsute Samson clutching a jawbone of an ass says, "Cease thy Philistine nagging, I'll get my hair cut when I want to." Ben's favorite showed the Prince of Denmark in black regalia, standing at a writing desk with a quill in hand. "No no no," he is penning, "what I said was, 'Get thee a new hummy bee.'"

They had sent out dozens of these cartoons without ever getting an acceptance or even encouragement, not even the Samson with her best ever drawing. Yet the whole process worked to add a distinctive flavor to the relationship. Ironically, because they could work at it while apart, it helped maintain their connection while they saw less and less of one another.

The drifting-apart became partly geographical when Sophie and Miriam decided to move uptown, renting a two-bedroom apartment on the Upper West Side, walking distance from the 92nd Street Y and the Lincoln Center (which they laughingly called the "epicenter of world culture"). The sisters had both changed jobs. Eighteen months at the publisher's shop were all Miriam needed to make the logical professional move into a literary agency (which proved over time to have launched a successful career). And almost simultaneously Sophie realized that her talents were better realized as a designer of books and their covers, and she filled a comfortable slot with a major publisher (one that disproved over time the street-smart wisdom that book-publishing was moribund).

The new apartment went condo but they were able to finance the transfer with a little help from the folks back home in Altoona. It was perfect for them, single professional women that they were. Each had her own bedroom and bath in an old building with ample space. The modest kitchen suited them; neither cared much for the culinary arts. And instead of a living room they set up home offices for their respective trades. It was not a place of social intercourse, but they enjoyed an active social life elsewhere. They were popular in each other's active circles, and an invitation to one always included the other. They were often referred to as the "Weiss-guys" for their quippy conversation, which seemed to work better in tandem than as solo artists. Meanwhile, in the privacy of their own domain they kidded each other as the "S and M sisters from Altoona," not entirely a private joke because their name-tag over their doorbell downstairs read "S. and M. Weiss."

Ben's cartoon ideas stopped coming to the new address, and

Sophie realized one day that she hadn't seen him in six months. The slight pang of loss was more than compensated for by the sense that she had only misplaced what she had never really owned. Her memories of him were pleasant, unlike those of his erstwhile friend William. The Siegel name turned up in the news on occasion, his hedge-fund manipulations being more public than those of most of his colleagues. He had never bothered her again, but when he went to trial for insider trading she celebrated his misfortune.

The last she heard of Ben came from her old friend Irv, who had consistently kept in touch, mostly with the local news from Altoona, where his OB-GYN practice had built upon his father's foundation. An incidental remark filled her in, though Irv apparently never had an inkling of the complications he had unwittingly and indirectly wrought upon her. Ben, he reported, had divorced his wife, had assumed exclusive custody of his children, and had accepted a senior position at the University of Alabama in Tuscaloosa.

Sophie was happy for him, glad too that she had kept her secret knowledge from him, her slightly awkward but fondly remembered first lover. During football season, to the bewilderment of everybody who knew her, she sometimes burst out with the chant: "Roll Tide!" Then finally she put it on her phone the year round at the end of the request for recorded messages. She never solved that cryptic puzzle for anyone, but took pride in the feeling that she was keeping faith with her lost love, a kind of private tribute to a cherished memory.

Zero-Grounded

He was almost back to his office in the World Trade Center, after his weekly breakfast meeting with Roger, his Wall Street bookie, when the first plane hit. Instinctively he reached for his cell phone, awkwardly easing it out of a pocket crammed with stacks of currency. For a second or two he hesitated, trying to decide whether to hit 1 on the speed dial for his wife at home in Scarsdale or 2 for his office on the 98th floor upstairs where he'd left his assistant just thirty minutes ago. On an impulse that would change his life, he did neither, turning back into the street.

He looked up for just an instant and walked away, oblivious of the screaming and shouting around him and the already frantic movements of people running in all directions. He walked slowly back toward the coffee shop on Broadway where Roger had made good on the biggest single payoff since he started betting on sports fifteen years ago.

Turning the corner, he realized he was still gripping that phone. He dropped it, stomped on it, and kicked it into the sewer. Nobody around him, in the growing street crowd and with the earliest responders arriving, seemed to notice. He didn't know what he was doing. He knew exactly what he was doing.

Much later, when he thought back to this first hour of his escape, he imagined a debate taking place in his subconscious. Part of him saw himself as the embodiment of loyal American values, a patriotic celebrant of the American Dream, the ideal of entrepreneurial success, an affluence adorned by the perfect family. Maintaining a competitive edge with hard work, he was a poster boy for the Protestant ethic. On the other side, perhaps disguised by his avocation for gambling, was another core set of American values, a longing for adventure, exploration, discovery, a life of solitary self-sufficiency as Pathfinder or Pioneer, a fantasy of riding alone on the frontier toward whatever might wait over the next ridge. It was this half-buried self-image, he rationalized later, that had prevailed, compelling him to take the opportunity offered and light out for the Territory.

The second plane flew into the South Tower as he began to walk uptown, and again he looked up only briefly before continuing at a steady pace up the east side of Broadway. He had never seen so many people on foot in lower New York. They weren't milling or swarming, but were moving purposefully in opposite directions— toward the scene and away from it. And a kind of street telegraph was operating, so that minute by minute he heard reports of what was going on, what little was known, what questions were gradually beginning to be answered. Without trying, he took it all in, listening with hypervigilant attention to what was being called out around him, while his mind was racing, randomly, far removed from the immediate scene.

All sorts of scattered thoughts flashed through his mind as he walked, all the while registering the bulletins as the street telegraph announced them. Terrorist attack. Rescue efforts. The South Tower collapsed. A couple of bars of an old song began playing in an endless loop in his head. When it became annoying, he became conscious of the lyric. It was, "Just walk away, Renee."

He forced himself to concentrate on Janet. She'd be terribly upset and anxious, but not hysterical. She was one of the steadiest, most resilient people he knew. She'd be fine. She was a lovely woman, everything he could want in a wife. She suited his tastes and met his needs. He loved her and had never been unfaithful. But it was clear he was thinking of her in the past tense, then shifting into the subjunctive mood. She would grieve but carry on, and she would certainly remarry, attractive as she was, while always putting the girls first.

He missed her already. And he could always go back, "recovering" from a "traumatic amnesia." The reunion would be wonderful, though the girls wouldn't understand it at all. They were not a factor in his thinking now, just as they had made little impact on his life. Two delightful little children twenty months apart, they had not connected with him in a meaningful way. He enjoyed watching them when he was around, but somehow he had yet to become an active force in their young lives. They wouldn't miss him, would hardly be aware that he was gone, and Janet would provide the continuity that would sustain them. And now they would be rich. He had provided well for contingencies, and he was sure there would be even greater inheritances coming their way in the wake of this, what, tragedy, calamity, atrocity? No, he wasn't going back. The Pentagon hit. A fourth plane crashed in Pennsylvania. The North Tower collapsed.

At Union Square he sat on a bench and began to make detailed plans—just in case he decided to go ahead with his impulsive escape, take it to the limit. A quotation from somewhere he couldn't place came into his head: "Anarchy is the fine line between chaos and freedom." Erase the line, he thought. Chaos had been imposed on his world. He could step out of it, cross over the line into a kind of freedom he had occasionally fantasized.

If he could break loose from the ties that bound him, setting aside mere material ambition, driven only to keep moving beyond imposed guidelines, fences, boundaries, and borders—without obligation— then he'd never regret a road not taken. Freedom had always meant equal opportunity to pile up winnings and measure your stack against others. But it had a stronger meaning for him now, the sense having nothing to lose. If he didn't jump at it, he'd be giving up the chance to see a new sun on a new day in a new place, beholden to none. His family, his country, his way of life, he could turn his back on it all, knowing that they didn't need him to survive. It may be a heavy sacrifice but he felt unburdened by remorse for making it.

Within half a block on Fourteenth Street he managed to get everything he needed in several shops. He chose a White Sox cap, avoiding a New York connection and knowing that a Cubs hat would invite conversation. Jeans, denim shirt, sweatshirt, cross-training shoes, sunglasses—an odd item for one who had never worn glasses of any kind. A duffel bag, to carry his dress clothes and shoes once he'd changed, until he could safely dispose of them, and to stash his cash, nine small stacks of five grand each in hundreds, while he carried the rest folded into his pocket.

Little more than half an hour later, he walked into a men's room at the Port Authority Bus Terminal, and when he came out he was a new man. He thought about heading for Monmouth Park, then laughed at the thought. He wasn't just taking a day off or cutting school to go gamble. He thought of Philadelphia Park, too, where he'd had some of his best days at the track, but when he bought his bus ticket for Philly it was for different reasons.

He could always go back. No one would doubt him or question how he had gotten to wherever he was. He simply couldn't remember anything after the plane hit the tower. The more clearly he recalled every detail of the morning, the more easily he could imagine forgetting it all.

Riding in the bus he distracted himself by thinking about Roger. He pictured him sitting in a deli with a bunch of his cronies, like the scene in "Broadway Danny Rose," only instead of comedians they were all bookies. And Roger was telling about the hit he took on 9/11, how he had just paid off one of his best customers with a huge payoff. He could do a dead-on imitation of Roger, often cracking up his friends with it, and now he could hear it in his head.

"This guy, big-time funds manager, one of the biggest fish in my pond, all of a sudden he can do no wrong. Starts right in on Tuesday, betting baseball. He's such a good customer and steady loser I give him the nickel line, and now he gets hot. Catches teams on streaks, bets Oakland every day and they keep winning, bets against Baltimore every day and they keep losing, Red Sox four out of five losers, Yankees, four out of five winners, Cubs five straight losers, Mets six straight winners. Most suckers will bet to end streaks, this guy all of a sudden figures out you can only win once that way but a streak can go on and on.

"This guy is a nickel-and-dime bettor, and we settle on ten dimes on Tuesdays if he's up or down—which he usually is most weeks for ten years. Plays parlays, teasers, over-and-under, I'm tellin' you, a born loser when it comes to sports. Now he's only making straight bets and winning almost all of 'em. Thursday night he comes in on a college football game, N.C. State for five dimes, and he's up fifteen dimes. Saturday bets three more college games same way, wins 'em all, Nebraska, Maryland, and Fresno fuckin' State—all big winners and he's up thirty.

"I'm not worried, this guy will always give it back, but Sunday he has six NFL games, ten dimes each. He only wins three but the other three are pushes, two of 'em in overtime. I don't know what he's doin', like he takes the invitation on the Chargers minus two and a half but goes the other way with the Dolphins plus six and a half. Monday night, are you kiddin' me? He sends it all in, sixty dimes on Denver. He wins and I have to pay him Tuesday morning, but I figure it'll all come back to me in time. All of a sudden he's the luckiest man in the world. And he walks into the tower with his pockets loaded with my money and burns up with the bills still hot in their wrappers."

He knew that Roger, like any gambler telling about bad beats, would naturally exaggerate the figure, more than double in this version, but he could afford it. Roger might have lost a few good customers, but at least he could dine out on this story for months, an ironic take on a national catastrophe, tailored to suit an audience of other gamblers.

In Philadelphia he got a shave and haircut. His full beard had covered his weak chin for a full dozen years, and his collar-length brown hair was now trimmed to marine-crew length. Only it wasn't brown and there was no trace of the reddish highlights. Looking in the barber's mirror he was only mildly surprised to see that his hair had turned white.

His next ticket was for San Diego. He was thinking Tijuana, but by the time they reached St. Louis he had changed his mind. And by then he had chosen his name. He hit on Wilson right away, from the red tennis bag a kid had carried onto the bus, but decided it was too common for a last name. He thought long and hard, eliminating everything that had even the slightest personal association, and came up with McKendry. Satisfied, he thought that he could use Mac, Wil, or Will for a nickname.

So it was Wilson McKendry who reached San Antonio, stashed most of his belongings in a locker, and took another bus west on I-10 into El Paso. Next morning he walked into Ciudad Juarez, oblivious of the lack of heightened vigilance at the border, with enough cash to get what he needed. It took barely half an hour to find the shop he was looking for, on the Avenue de Palmas just off 16 de Septembre, and two hours later he had exchanged fifteen Ben Franklins for some high-quality documents (you get what you pay for, his father had always said)—driver's license, social security card, and passport. Properly (apparently) stamped, the latter was cursorily checked as he walked back into El Paso across the Stanton Bridge after an overnight "pleasure trip," returned to San Antonio, picked up his duffel, and rented a car before checking into a different motel.

New self, new life. Let freedom ring. Janet would be fine. The girls would be fine. And he would be free. The cash he had was woefully inadequate as a stake for the lifestyle he craved, but once he had an identity and a laptop he knew it wouldn't matter. As long as he stayed away from places where he might be recognized, he was home free. Home? Where the action was—it had nothing to do with the heart. Internet betting and day-trading, living by his wits, making what he needed and no more, in other words, working (hah! it was playing!), but only when he wanted to.

He slept soundly but woke early and drove up to Austin for two reasons: to do some research in one of the great libraries in the world and to buy a laptop in a market where there was substantial turnover from student trade. By the end of the day he had his equipment and was also equipped with a plan of action that would get him back in action. In particular he had an immediate destination. Since he had to have a bank account before he could establish betting accounts and trading accounts, he decided to go where he could find all three, the Caymans.

George Town on Grand Cayman seemed made to order for him, busy but not too overcrowded, touristy but with tourism taking second place to banking and trading in its economy. He could blend in here more easily than in someplace more remote or exotic. A couple of days in the Holiday Inn were all he needed to get acclimated, set up his accounts, and find a bungalow to rent near the outer end of Seven Mile Beach. The limit of six months residence would hardly be a problem, he knew, and he planned to do more traveling anyway.

Now, with a place to live and a local address for his accounts, he could begin to do what he had been craving, living the kind of active life that defined freedom for him. There were opportunities galore in the plunging market, but he lacked the bankroll to take full advantage. He could only play in a small way and so took great care to single out his choices.

The sports action was different. As long as he kept winning, his accounts steadily growing, he could have the constant stimulation and instant gratification of clever handicapping. What pleased him so much was not the winning itself, certainly not the size of his bets (he wasn't about to risk big chunks of his modest bankroll), nor even the fact of being in action—unlike most habitual bettors, he no longer felt that the next best thing to betting and winning was betting and losing. No, in fact, what delighted him was the almost smug satisfaction of knowing when not to bet, of avoiding, for example, the "invitations" that clever lines-makers issued every week during the football season, not to mention the so-called thrill of college basketball where a betting result would hinge on whether a teenage sub would make a free throw in the final seconds. He studied patterns, gathered information, and did comparison shopping for the best point spreads. He was selective and confident. And he won, with a consistency that gave him enough income for his immediate needs and saw his accounts grow steadily if unspectacularly.

He followed the sports and financial news carefully, other news only casually, though he did take particular note of the shrinking death toll from the atrocity. They'd never have an accurate count, not if they counted him, but he did wonder where they had found all those survivors from the early estimates. And he took in some of the personal stories, like the guy in the Pentagon who had called a meeting for his staff of 35, been late getting there himself for the first time in his punctilious career, and found them all wiped out at impact.

He imagined Janet dutifully posting photos of him all over lower Manhattan, holding on to faint hope against hope, once it became clear that no verifiable trace of his remains would emerge. The only one who might respond to the picture and plea would be Roger, but there were long odds against that. And what could Roger say, that they had had breakfast together and he was heading back to his office just in time for the first hit?

He would gaze out to sea at different hours of daylight and dark, pondering the meaning of survivor guilt. He understood the burden of being the one marked for protection from the angel of death, when others perished, whether strangers or family or, as in his case, all of his colleagues. No one on his floor had gotten out. The one who was blessed could be cursed by the feeling that he had been spared for some special purpose, the weight of responsibility to justify his luck, and the frustration of knowing he could never live up to such spotlighted expectations.

On the other hand, why not think of survival from calamity as an opportunity, the chance of a new lifetime? What's wrong with taking advantage of good fortune, of making the most of things, of emerging from calamity with new resolve and good intentions, of finding a silver lining in the blackest of clouds? Gift horses need to be ridden, not scrutinized and analyzed for flaws. A breakdown, a therapist friend had once told him, is sometimes a break-through, a new beginning, a cracking of a shell to emerge into the light newly enlightened.

His original estimate, based on what he knew of a busy day in the Towers, was that 20,000 people would have been killed. As the estimates dropped below a fourth of that, his relief came with surprise, though he grieved for the hundreds of victims he knew, people he used to see almost every day. But he was sure that they would never have an accurate total. Some people besides him would have walked away. The way he saw it, though, the others would be people dissatisfied with their lives, over-anxious from the rat race, depressed by debt, burdened by responsibilities, mired in dead-end jobs, trapped in unfulfilling or disastrous relationships.

Not him. He enjoyed his work, managing institutional portfolios, pleasing his big-hitter clients, out-earning most of his colleagues at a prestigious firm. As a short-seller he had a gift for sniffing out over-valued or emptily inflated companies before they crashed, and in a volatile market he often spotted surefire bargains as well. He had actually moved into position to run his own hedge fund, a long-held ambition that could have been attained before his next birthday.

Nor was his marriage one to escape from. No complaints on either side, though there had been a time when Janet was uncomfortable with his habitual betting on sports. An admirable companion, a compatible sex partner, an attractive adornment to his entire domestic existence, Janet was the perfect wife for him. If he was walking away from her, he must be crazy—unless he was walking away from the very concept of "wife." In time, he knew there would be women, but he was in no hurry. And he was sure there would be no one woman. No one could touch what he'd had in Janet, but he'd had that and given it up, so what would be the point?

In the last week of October the dreams began. Innocuous enough at first, they generally had him in a familiar, comfortable, not unpleasant place. A beach, a wooded glade, the paddock at what he knew somehow was Narragansett Park, or a big bright exuberant casino he understood to be in Havana—though he was too young to have ever been in either of those two. He would be enjoying himself, begin to feel tired, and try to leave—only to be frustrated at every attempt to find his way out. The frustration built in an agonizing crescendo through anxiety toward panic. And when he came suddenly awake he was gasping for breath, heart racing, sweat cold and clammy on his arms and chest.

He recognized them as trap-and-escape dreams and put them down to a kind of vicarious post-traumatic stress. After all, he had never gotten trapped in the tower, had simply walked away without any struggle to escape. Falling back on his favorite defenses of rationalization and intellectualization, he managed to reason his way out of any troubling residual effects of the dreams.

And yet something strange and inexplicable began to take place. The visual images of the dreams would quickly fade in the rational light of day, but other sensations persisted. There was a constant roar in his ears, not tinnitus as he understood it, but sounds he recognized as a thunder of falling rubble accompanied by shrieking people. He had the feeling that his mouth was choked with dust, and his nose was filled with it to the point that he felt like he was breathing dust and rubble all day. And his eyes burned and repeatedly teared up with the acrid sting of smoldering ruins.

He could swim in the crystal clear Caribbean waters and not wash these sensations away. Yet there was no memory component to them. He had missed all that, walked away from it, deliberately avoided thinking about those who had experienced it.

He remembered a technique he'd heard about for dealing with recurrent nightmares. The idea was to instruct yourself, before going to sleep, to change one specific concrete element of the dream. It could be anything, a color, an item in a setting, the identity of a character— the point being to demonstrate some ability to have control over the unconscious dreaming self. One of two results almost always occurred. Either the dream would change (as instructed, suggesting that other changes could be made) or it would simply fail to recur.

He tried it, and it worked. The dream, even the whole underlying trap-and-escape structure, disappeared. Yet still he would wake with dry mouth, breathing and tasting dust, eyes smarting. He learned to control those sensations by focusing on activities, whether recreational or vocational, physical exercise or gambling and speculating, until all that remained of the after-effects was the dull roar of the mental soundtrack—and even that he managed to reduce to a kind of white noise, a reminder of who he was and how he got to where he was. Wilson McKendry was his own man, in control of his life, and enjoying the living of it.

Besides, if he wanted to, he could give up being Wilson McKendry. He could find his way home. The amnesia option was always there, like a cliché of soap opera story-arcs.

He had thought about Costa Rica, contemplated a travel itinerary that would take him and his laptop around the world, and then decided to put off any trip until after the first of the year, when he wanted to test the option of a summery winter down under. Then, maybe next winter in Buenos Aires, going up to Rio for Carnival. For now, he was comfortable in the Caymans, becoming a familiar figure on his morning runs and almost daily walk from his beach bungalow into town. There was a park where young men and teenagers played basketball on hard pavement and tin backboards, and he sometimes stopped and shot hoops with them, gradually being accepted as a regular and sometimes chosen for sides. When his old reliable jumper came back, he was not shy about calling "next" himself, and a number of the regular players were happy to play with "Mac."

No one would recognize him. He hardly recognized himself: white hair kept cropped youthfully short, clean-shaven, skin deeply tanned and creased from the Caribbean sun. He enjoyed preparing most of his own meals. He was, by God, as healthy as he'd ever been. He even went to a dentist, primarily to establish a dental-records identity, and learned he had no sign of decay. If this be mid-life crisis, make the most of it, he thought, though forty was still some birthdays away—on a date he'd invented for the purpose, and not 9/11. How many people would recognize 1/27 as Mozart's birthday?

He began spending evenings at Rosiez, where he was known as Will. This was a local hangout, a plain square board-tin-and-thatch building away from the beach, where tourists were a rare if not endangered species. No fishing nets or billowing sails or tequila sunrises decorated the walls, no spearfishing and snorkeling equipment in the ambience or décor. The familiar faces in Rosiez, mostly faces of color, belonged to indigenous working-class folks along with expatriates who were as likely to be from India or China as from the States or Cuba. Some of them made Will think of people wasting away in Margaritaville, even though the staple drink of the regulars was rum, which was poured at Rosiez from an ample variety of white, gold, and dark. No frozen daiquiris here.

If there had ever been a Rosie, she was long-gone, and the two current proprietors, Clifford and Spencer, alternated nights behind the bar. Like most of their customers, Cliff and Spence enjoyed casual, easy-going conversation on the staple topics of sports, weather, women, jobs, and local gossip. No politics or policy, no partisan exuberance, no disputes—a congenial but quiet place for steady but not serious drinkers. No sacred ginmill, no blues-and-jukebox atmosphere, no jailhouse jive.

No TV either. Will had learned long ago not to watch games he bet on, not to bet on games he knew he'd be watching. While betting on games enriched the experience for many spectators, for Will the bets distorted his sports-fan enjoyment. If he spent two or three hours a day following the markets and shopping for betting lines on his computer, that was more than enough screen-watching for him.

Only when his new life was threatened did he actually think of it as a fantasy idyll. And that threat came in a surprising form, in late December, when another mellow evening at Rosiez was interrupted by what felt to him like a harpoon in the gut. A half dozen young men had walked into the bar, their cut-off-jeans-and-sloganed-teeshirt look preceded by the sound of their roistering voices. Why are they coming here? was his first thought. His second was, Oh shit, because he recognized Royce Carlsen right away.

And he instantly knew why Royce and his friends were there. They weren't just bored college kids on Christmas break, looking for someplace different, somewhere not Lauderdale or Cancun. They were diving enthusiasts who wanted to visit Stingray City. And of all the rum joints in all the world.... Dick Carlsen was his friend and neighbor in Scarsdale, a TV network executive with whom he often commuted. Janet and Kathleen had become close, too, and the oldest Carlsen kid, Royce, had been their first babysitter when the girls were infants. Now here he was, the all-American responsible towhead teenager, sun-burnt and beer-glowed, looking, as it happened, for tips from the locals on best available boats and guides for their dives.

There was no ducking out, no escape from discovery. Will was about to be busted. His house of cards was about to be shattered by a missile from another country. Royce and his buddies chatted amiably and with some welcome deference with Cliff and some of the regulars at the bar. Then they sort of fanned out around the room, taking an informal canvas of the whole crowd. It was Royce himself who came to the table where Will was sitting, sipping quietly with Arjun, a congenial white-haired Indian whose smooth skin suggested he was of an age with Will.

"You are barking up the wrong tree here," Arjun said, in grinning answer to Royce's opening gambit. "We are living near the sea but are not being of the sea."

Will felt pierced by Royce's blue eyes as they turned to him. "Isn't that a waste of wonderful opportunities?" he said.

The pause before his answer was brief, hardly noticeable, yet felt momentous to Will. He wanted to greet the boy, wanted to hug him even, to tell him how good it was to see him, wanted to say, Don't you recognize me? And he expected to hear Royce say his name, express his shock, stammer out something like, We thought you were dead.

Instead, there was neither the slightest flicker of recognition nor a momentary narrowing of the eyes in suspicion or doubt. Unclouded blue like those Caribbean skies. And so he said, at last, "Depends what you mean by waste—and what you mean by opportunity."

Royce laughed and turned away, rejoining his buddies, and soon they were gone, just one beer and out the door in their carefree quest. I am no longer who I was, Will thought. The hair, the face, the glasses, the tan—it had all worked, and maybe the voice has changed, too, because Royce had heard it and no bells or alarms had rung.

Later than usual, he walked slowly back to his bungalow that night. He had aced a test, a tougher one than he ever thought he'd have to face, with colors flying high in a celebration of freedom achieved. "Home free," he thought, was an oxymoron. If you go home, you give up being free. He had crossed the finishing line from chaos to freedom. He could still go back, could reclaim his abandoned identity, could emerge with recovered memory of his pre-traumatized self—with a claim of amnesia for the interval that would withstand any challenge.

But to take that option was to close the circle, to give up on options. To go on was to keep that option open—along with limitless others. There were playoff games to handicap and opportunities to explore in a recovering market. There were places he wanted to go that he might never see. As long as the broken circle could be mended, he could go wherever the tangents took him. By-and-by, Lord, by-and-by, he hummed to himself as he lay down to sleep his dreamless night away.

Payback

The news of Peter Rondo's death must have shocked the millions for whom he was an icon and an idol. Obituaries, tributes, appreciations, and personal reminiscences led the news on TV and in the papers for several days and would turn up in magazine formats for weeks and even months to come. For my brother Tim and me, however, the reaction was different because he and Rondo had a personal history; I had heard Tim tell the story many times.

I called Tim as soon as I heard the news. I knew that he, ears tuned to news and gossip along the Rialto in the Manhattan he would never leave, would have heard it first, and I wanted to see how he was taking it. They had been classmates at the Yale Drama School back in the late Fifties, and for years Tim had dined out, or more accurately drunk out, on his Rondo story, the thesis of which was that he, Tim, had launched Peter Rondo on his illustrious career.

We all knew that Rondo's superior talent, his ruggedly handsome looks, those deeply compelling baby-blues, and his many fan-endearing accomplishments were sure to make him a big star anyway, but Tim's was a tale of origins, always good material in the arena and aura of stardom. What happened between them came before Rondo's early emergence on Broadway, before his move to Hollywood and the spectacular success of movie after movie—a dozen Oscar nominations over three decades.

It also came long before he married his equally talented and photogenic co-star, Annie Fullerton, long before they built their home back east in Greenwich where they lived between gigs and where Peter died, long before in mid-life he acquired the competitive tennis skills that allowed him to become a nationally ranked senior player, long before he developed a line of personally designed casual men's-wear products that he sold online with all receipts going to help support his non-profit foundation.

You may remember that Rondo's first break came when he read for the lead in a new Robert Flange play called "Barbecue." He had been bitterly disappointed when the part went to Stu Picker, an established leading man of that era. But Rondo had been cast in a supporting role and was also assigned to understudy Picker. You may recall, as well, the stuff of theatrical legend, those rave reviews Rondo earned the night he filled in for the suddenly incapacitated leading man. Tim's story was the back-story, a backstage back-story if there ever was one, of how that debut came to pass.

I am, literally if not literarily, writing this down, but it is my brother's story and I am merely his Boswellian amanuensis here. Tim and Rondo had stayed in touch after leaving New Haven, patronizing the same Village bars, trading tales of their frustrations in the quest to make it to the Great White Way, Tim as playwright, Rondo as actor, while jollying each other with the dream that one day they would work together. The night Rondo got that part in "Barbecue," Tim had been at the Village party celebrating the achievement—a minor role but a major breakthrough. But after that it was two months into the run before Tim heard from Rondo again, and here's where his story begins.

The phone rang, and my brother heard that distinctive voice say, "Tim, let's get together for drinks tomorrow afternoon."

"What's the occasion, Peter?"

"Nothing special. We haven't traded Red Warren or Frank Gilroy stories in a long time, and I've got some new stuff for you to hear.

Two o'clock at Menotti's, okay? It'll be on me, Tim—I'm the one with the gig."

My brother showed up early and ordered a light lunch, in part to lay claim to a booth for them, which turned out to be a good idea when right on time Peter Rondo made his entrance accompanied by none other than Stu Picker. After a manly introductory handshake, the star slid into the booth followed by his understudy. They all seemed to hit it off and chatted pleasantly, Tim sipping a martini, Peter nursing the house Chianti, and Picker, who was famously on the wagon, tossing off a Schweppes with a twist.

At this point I would ask what they had talked about. Depending on who else was in his audience, Tim would sometimes give a generalized response like, "Oh, shared familiar experiences, meaning we traded lies about ourselves." But sometimes he'd say, "Mostly we joked about us being together, you know, three straight men of the theater drinking together of an afternoon in Greenwich Village, just around the corner from Stonewall."

"Not that there's anything wrong with it"—my well-rehearsed line.

"Right, but we called ourselves the 'Anomalous Trio'—which was not only braggadocio but a joke in itself, because during our time at Menotti's both Hoffman and Cassavetes had crossed those sawdust-covered floorboards in hot pursuit of targets of their customary skirt-chasing. The place was known for it. After 'Kiss Me Kate' opened, they thought about changing the name to 'Cremona.'"

"Why 'Cremona'?" I'd always say, on cue.

"Don't you remember? 'Lots of quail in Cremona.'"

In any event the three of them were small-talking their way through a couple of drinks. After about an hour, Peter excused himself to go to the loo (as he called it, without apparent irony)—and didn't come back to the booth. Tim expressed no surprise, shrugging his shoulders when Picker said, "What's he up to?" And shortly thereafter,

Stu Picker delivered his trademark line, "Ah, fuck it," and ordered himself a boilermaker.

Suddenly the light-bulb lit up in the balloon over Tim's head as he realized that Peter had set them both up, the lead player in "Barbecue" and the understudy's reliable buddy. If Picker could be induced to have a drink, he wouldn't be able to stop, and who would be better able to drink right along with him than good old Tim. At least, he thought, Rondo had the good grace not to tell him in advance of the canny plot, so that he'd never have to feel like an un-indicted co-conspirator.

So Tim played his part as Rondo had written it, and so did Stu Picker who proceeded through the afternoon to drink himself into a state of incoherent, falling-down sloshedness. Here my brother regularly performed one of his original pieces of shtick, his impression of the several states of inebriation. He called it his "Seven Stages of Drinking Man" routine, as if Shakespeare's Jaques were channeling Chaucer's Miller.

Anyway, this was all build-up and delay and mounting suspense for the punch line or punch-drunk climax of the story. Because the rest is theatrical history; that was the night Peter Rondo made his debut as a leading man on Broadway, the proverbial emergency stand-in who earns accolades, receives offers galore, and quicksteps to fame and fortune. He never made a false step looking back.

"Peter had planned it well," Tim always said with a savvy look. "He had suggested to his newly-signed agent that the Broadway beat reporters be tipped off that Picker would be replaced by Rondo that night. But it all depended on me playing Falstaff, drinking right along with the Prince. And that's how I launched the flight of Rondo's career."

That's how Tim usually ends his story, adding his wry anti-climax, "And he's never said thank you. In fact, I've never heard from him since."

So I called my brother and said. "Are you mourning the loss?"

"No more than for any other fallen popular hero."

"Well, I've gone on-line to read as many obits as I can find, Tim, and every one of them talks about that dramatic beginning in the Flange play. But not a one mentions how he got to go on that night. Isn't this the time to tell your story again? To reach the audience you deserve?"

"No," he said, "I've gotten all the mileage I can out of that one, closed the book and lyrics long ago."

"But you were a good friend, even to the point of doing for him something that must have seemed very distasteful to you after the fact. And he never even thanked you."

"I guess it goes into the no-good-deed-goes-unpunished file."

"Well, before you file it away for keeps, I think this is the time and the opportunity for a little payback."

Tim's voice got a little hesitant, then, as it does when he's trying to figure out if I'm serious or playing with him. "What do you mean?"

"Well, Annie's sitting up there in her widow's weeds in that lush but understated showplace in Greenwich, you know, the traditional lifestyle that took the Village out of Greenwich. She may be grieving but she's still beautiful after all these years. Tim, she's never even met the man who got her beloved husband his big start. I think you owe it to her to call, or, better, go see her. Really, you owe it to yourself. Express your condolences—and tell her your own exclusive Peter Rondo story. She'll laugh. She'll cry. She's an actress-widow, after all.

"Move right in, Tim. It's only fair. After all he was blessed with because of what you did for him, you should reap some of the benefits. It would be a marriage made in a just world and a payback heaven."

I didn't hear him laugh, but I could envision him sitting there with a grin on his relatively unlined faced, lighting up that rent-controlled Murray Hill studio, staging in his mind a fantasy scene. He would never act it out, I knew. What's more, he'd never even write the scene. Would he send a sympathy note, maybe signed "Secret

Admirer"? No, not my brother, the silent, unrequited sufferer. But none of that inhibits my determination to tell his story. He's my muse for this one, and I'm his devoted and friendly ghost.

Call me Casper.

One Thing and Another

First

At exactly ten minutes before noon, the stentorian voice of Chester D. Southey boomed out his monosyllabic call to his comrades in arms, the other senior members in the department. "Lunch" resounded through the department corridors, and three or four of his posse would quickly assemble and escort him on the short walk to the Faculty Club where a table was reserved for them.

Keith sat in his office and smiled at the way he could set his watch by the Southey summons. He also knew that another gathering, of younger staff, would be taking place over the next half hour as his junior colleagues informally headed for their favorite watering hole just off campus--a rather raucous, up-beat group of variable numbers enjoying clever conversation, even when rehearsed.

Keith would not be joining them this time. The door to his office was closed. He was eating a brown-bag lunch while trying to grade a few papers and had scheduled a couple of conferences with students at 12:15 and 12:45. But thirty years after the fact Keith would still remember what he heard that day, not just the words but the sound of the voices uttering them, not to mention the sequence of his own reactions to them.

It was the joking voice of Tim Myers, probably the wittiest of the young Turks, clearly resonating, in an easy-going drawl utterly without malice: "Anyone who sleeps with Martha Johnson would have to be crazy."

The first thing that occurred to Keith was that the remark was directed at him, since it had become apparent that Martha had fallen into the habit of visiting him in his office on the days when the graduate courses she was taking met in the seminar rooms upstairs. At first it had been a bit of a nuisance to him. She had no particular reason to single him out; she had never been his student, he was not on her thesis committee, and her concentration on the Protestantism of nineteenth-century American writers was totally removed from his own fields of interest. But gradually their conversations, turning to matters of popular culture and politics, had become more comfortable, even pleasantly congenial.

So, no, he quickly rejected the gut reaction that it was about him and instead felt insulted on her behalf. Martha was not an attractive woman. Her mousy demeanor, unflattering clothes, slouching posture, whiny voice, and mouth full of misaligned teeth all told might make one wonder what her husband had ever seen in her. Keith, for his part, appreciated the intelligence she could not hide and her tastes in matters literary and cinematic. At first shyly and then proudly she'd show him reviews she had written for local newspapers and magazines. So there had developed something simpatico between them, having nothing to do with the terminal nature of his own disastrous marriage nor with the personal history she would eventually share with him.

And then, in the quiet of the lunch-emptied corridor, he fearfully entertained the notion that the Myers wit had been directed at the unlikely and frightening discovery that he and Martha had in fact begun an affair. He was, however, not stricken with fear so much as triggered to anger. He wanted to shout at Tim that he was an ignorant fool, that Martha Johnson had revealed to him a beauty beyond any he had beheld--or held.

Her rural upbringing had been dominated by a tyrannical father and influenced by a cravenly submissive mother, who shared a belief that pride was indeed the deadliest of all sins. And that core belief translated into aversion to all forms of personal vanity. Hence the posture, the apparel, the total absence of anything suggestive of makeup or decoration or appearance, not to mention orthodontics. Her physical features were as God intended them to be; anything that would make her more attractive physically was vile and would warrant physical beatings. Moreover, anything that drew attention to a superior intellect or that would encourage educational ambition was equally abhorrent.

She had barely graduated high school when she agreed to marry a man who shared her parents' beliefs in general, including especially the prohibition of vanity, but with a grudging agreement to "allow" her to continue her education. She understood that this was a practical accommodation, so that in time she could pursue some kind of professional employment that would make the marriage economically feasible. He was a "scientist," after all, with a bachelor's degree in engineering, who could rationalize her intellectual ambitions as long as there was no trace of physical vanity. He wouldn't agree to let her get her teeth fixed either.

Keith took all this in with a growing sense that there was a major dose of pity in his feelings about her. Or for her. And when he put his arms around her that first time in his office, she cried with gratitude. It pleased him that he could so simply satisfy some of her need, some buried wish for a personal identity outside the strictures of her imposed way of life. So it was not, he had persuaded himself, just another way for him to fill his own needs; he could do that elsewhere, if not at home, and sometimes did.

They talked about what had happened and what was happening, at length and with candor, for several weeks, until they arranged to meet at an out-of-the-way motel. And that was where and when he was surprisingly awed by her beauty. Naked, she shed all the outer accouterments of her modesty, her unattractiveness, her repressed self. Her body was exquisite, perfect, he thought, and he told her so. She responded with a passion that seemed to him instinctive, and they gratified themselves and each other in ways that demanded that they meet again.

And again. And yet again. Four times all told, with equal satisfaction and appreciation, and then it was over. "I just wanted to know what it would be like, needed to know," she said. "Not just what I could be, but what I was."

She thanked him, saying she'd always remember what they had, that it would strengthen and enrich her throughout her life. And he thanked her in turn, with a promise of cherishing his memory of her, never to be shared with anyone. He would never indulge the temptation to tell Tim Myers how wrong he had been to insult her in his casual way.

She stopped visiting his office, though she continued to send him her reviews whenever they appeared, at least for a couple of years. By then, when he had moved on to another campus and finally ended the torment of a misguided marriage, the reprints stopped coming. But the memory lingered, recurred, never lost its power, its immediacy. Most of all it served as a point, not of departure, but measurement. It confirmed a habit of appreciation, a quality he took some private pride in, and he felt somehow identified by it, strengthened, confirmed.

Second

Between marriages, Keith would deliberately invoke that memory, even in the most unlikely situations where he could acknowledge that it was more of a rationalization than a justification. For example, there was the flirtation with Pretty, the young Jamaican woman he actually met when she served him at the lunch-counter of a shopping mall. Laughing to himself about the cliché of trying to pick up a waitress, he used her name-tag to initiate a conversation, knowing that she must have heard it a hundred times--despite her age and apparent lack of experience.

"You don't need to draw attention to the way you look," he said.

"But that's my name," she said, smiling, with that musical lilt he had always admired in Caribbean accents. And then he watched her walk away, swinging her hips in a manner he had always appreciated as a mark of Caribbean style even while disclaiming the racial profiling he deplored.

He sat there much longer than his b.l.t. called for, and she kept smiling at him, until he decided he had to say something more.

"Which island is it where those green eyes come from?" was his weak line, but he had really been strongly taken by their sparkling brightness.

"Jamaica," she said, still smiling, but neither encouraging nor dismissive. "Ocho Rios."

"I wish I could take you over to Negril for a drink at Rick's after work," he said.

"Too far a drive for a drink," she said, not bothering to acknowledge that he knew something about her island home.

But Keith felt somehow encouraged and quickly said, "When you have a break, can we talk some more?"

"Sure," she said, somehow making a song of the syllable and dancing away down the counter.

So he strolled around the mall, stopping back at her station to check on when she'd be free, and finally they strolled together for ten minutes while he followed the script he'd been rehearsing to establish a connection, to play out his fantasy of a pick-up dream come true. Inwardly laughing at himself for what he was doing, he pursued a strategy of getting her to tell him her story. And the openness of her narration, renewed two hours later in another ten-minute chapter, was music, or rather a song and dance, to his ears and eyes.

When he invited her to have dinner with him later, he framed it as a way to hear, in the Paul Harvey catch-phrase, "the rest of the story." She agreed and he was back to meet her at 7:30.

Everything about Pretty was easy-going and upbeat. Her smile was constant but at the same time seemed unrehearsed and authentic. The very music of her voice smoothed over any element of surprise, like when she told him, without any apparent prompting, that she wasn't as young as he probably thought, that she was far from being a silly teen-ager. How that translated into actual numbers Keith neither assumed nor cared. She simply was letting him know that going with the flow was her guiding principle and that to be with her he would have to join her in that regard. It came so readily that he accepted it with a kind of gratitude that he hoped had the effect of congeniality and comfortable engagement.

It took no more than a single question to open her up to a candid summary of her present situation and what had led her here. "I'm staying with a bunch of cousins here, a crowded three-bedroom apartment" she began, and he understood immediately that the import of this preamble had to do with where he would not be welcome to go, for one thing, and for another, that the follow-up question would not be "Your place or mine" but "Would you like to see where I live?" He also knew that he could take his time before offering that invitation, feeling certain for no obvious reason that she would accept it.

"I made a reservation at El Siboney," he said, "and I took the liberty of ordering the paella in advance."

"Perfect," she said, "as long as you'll drive me home so I can change clothes first."

Her apartment building was not far, and he waited in the car for the ten minutes it took her to change into a simple flowery dress, with no make-up he could detect, and she was carrying a large bag, big enough, he thought, that it might contain another change of clothes and a tooth brush. Everything about her flowed so smoothly into his fantasy that he had to warn himself to slow down, trying to match the easy and nonchalant pace of her manner.

As soon as she had ordered her Mojito, she picked up her tell-all narrative: "I've only been here a few months, but I couldn't stand to stay on the island with those parents of mine any longer. My momma is an obeah woman, proud of it, throwing her weight around in all directions--except at her husband--and making as many enemies as friends. I've seen that she has powers, but she's probably crazy. Papa is a mean old man, known in our village and around, and acts as if he's free to interfere with children, boys and girls, whenever he wants and before they even know what's going on."

"You said 'They' but do you mean 'We'?" he asked, surprising himself that he could ask such an intrusive question and believe she would find nothing judgmental toward her in it.

"Yes," she said, still smiling. "I was abused along with my brothers and sisters before me, and all my cousins. That's what we mean by 'interfered.' There isn't anyone in my apartment here that doesn't know, first-hand, what I've been through."

"I like the use of 'first-hand' in that," he said, and she laughed.

"Sometimes I like to play with words," she said. Then, "I have a feeling that's irie with you."

"Yes, I like to play, too, and not just with words, and I hope that's irie with you." Keith had surprised himself again, not only for being so uncharacteristically forward with this young Pretty but because he felt so comfortable doing it.

He found the Pretty face grinning broadly at him, and she reached across the table to touch his hand. There was neither embarrassment nor subtlety in the way she regarded him, and though conversation lagged while they attended to their seafood with black beans and yellow rice there was no awkwardness in the silence they comfortably shared.

Two Mojitos, a delicious meal, and a charmingly open woman not much more than half his age, made Keith feel as if he was cruising on some sweet ganja. They skipped dessert and he drove her, no questions asked, straight to his apartment. With the same rhythmic grace that had turned him on earlier she walked straight to the shelves of books and CDs that flanked his old-fashioned stereo. He rejected the knee-jerk notion to put on one of his Bob Marleys, slipping his favorite

Gregory Isaacs into the slot. She responded as he'd hoped beyond hope she would and said, "Our own 'Mr. Cool' himself," saying it as if she might have been ambiguously praising him. Again she seemed to accept his Jamaican point of reference without question

Pretty began to dance, beckoned him to join her, and he felt transported to a magic island. The next hour was a dream. They danced, embraced, and kissed. She began to take off clothes, his as well as hers, slowly but surely. And it was she who led him into his own bedroom, where he experienced an arousal that was more sensuous without the distraction of passion than he'd ever known.

When she left in the morning, it was as if it had all been scripted, a chapter in her own narrative, with the assumption that it would carry over to the next. "I'll see you tonight," she said, "and I'll bring our supper."

Keith could hardly believe his luck. He wondered how he could have won the lottery when he had never bought a ticket. This, he knew, could not last, but he determined that he would just enjoy it for all it was worth as long as it lasted. And he would relax and let Pretty do as she would with him. *Yes,* he thought, *Pretty is as Pretty does.*

The whole paradise cruise lasted just short of a week. "I have to go home," she told him on their sixth night together. "I've had a call from my brother that Momma is sick, and I have to go."

They talked for hours, as she told him of her mixed feelings toward her mother, not only about her refusal or inability to deal with her husband's evil ways but her ways of imposing harsh if not demonic punishments on others, including her own children. Keith wondered if she'd ever come back, but without talking about that he cautiously suggested that this trip might be an opportunity for her to confront her father. "I'll be in touch" was the last thing she said to him, and Keith wondered not so much whether she meant it but how she would fulfill the promise.

The answer arrived in a gaudily flowered envelope three weeks later. "Momma died," she wrote in a broad, almost childish hand.

"Nobody's mourning, but I have to stay here. Nobody else can take care of Papa, even if they wanted to. I know he doesn't deserve me, but he's a helpless old man and at least I can make sure he doesn't ever interfere with any child again--if I have to tie him up." Then, a brief p.s.: "Thanks for our week together. Remember me kindly, Pretty."

He did as she asked. She didn't have to ask. And he remembered her pretty, and the music and dance of her fondly.

Third

Coming up on the winter break, just starting to emerge from a depressive episode, Keith booked a trip to Aruba. Not a gambling junket, he thought, though he might try his luck at the casino tables once or twice while he was there; to distance himself from that action he chose a beach hotel not quite walking distance from the Marriott. He had some books to read, a few writing projects to play around with, and a paperback of various word and number puzzles. He looked forward to relaxing in a shack-for-one at the waterfront with its own private hot tub facing the water, and he was pleased to plan on avoiding any New Year's celebration.

He had been to the Caribbean a few times before, though he had no interest in any sport or activity associated with the water. He went there always in part to escape the winter cold, was always affronted by the ubiquitous displays of poverty, usually enjoyed good island cuisine and the upbeat crowds of merry-making tourists from around the world, and sometimes reveled in playing tennis on the red clay courts he adored. But this would be his first visit to the Dutch Antilles, and he knew that whatever decent food he'd find would likely be imported from Venezuela, that even the seafood was likely to be frozen, but that the fruit and drinking water were no risks to his system.

The idea was to be alone and to enjoy a rare spell of solitude, to get comfortable in his own skin, to be away from whatever had been contributing to his stinking, sinking mood. He was sure this trip would be tonic--relaxing and re-invigorating. It helped his choice of destination that the big boom (or bubble) of luxury resorts had yet to arrive on the island, which ten years later might be the last place he'd think of as an escape from whatever had been crowding his lifestyle and clouding his affect.

At the airport he went out of his way to pick up whatever tourist-guide material he could find, especially a detailed map of the island and its meager tourist attractions. Later that night his attention was caught by a flimsy hand-out touting the "wild parakeets" of Aruba. The text, in wikipedic fashion, listed the common varieties of bird life a visitor might see--Bananaquit, Carib Grackle, Crested Caracara, Ruddy Turnstone, and Yellow Warbler--and then bragged about the wild parakeets (Aratinga Pertinax) that flocked and roosted every night at sundown in the cliffs along the shore at the highest point on Aruba.

Keith had never been accused of being a bird-watcher. Indeed wild life, for him, meant the wandering ways of his youth, nothing to do with avian acquisitiveness--though he had known colleagues who kept records of their sightings on sabbatical excursions.

Somehow, though, this clumsy little flyer triggered an urge for something rare and different. So the next afternoon he drove across the island in his rental to that set of cliffs along the western shore and parked in an empty lot in solitary expectation of the advertised spectacle.

At other places in vacation-world, crowds would gather to applaud the sunsets, but here he was alone in a silence and absence that was in its way as stunning as it was soothing. And then the sun began to dip just below the horizon and suddenly hundreds of birds congregated along the cliffside, filling the air with a sound that was more a roar than a tweet. No, not hundreds. Thousands. And the sound of it was overwhelming. It was all he could do not to shout out an ooh and an ah the way galleries do at impressive fireworks or audiences do at Cirque de Soleil.

And then just as suddenly, as the sun disappeared entirely, it was silent again. The birds had disappeared, too, as if swallowed up by the cliff itself. Keith blinked in amazement. He had never seen or heard anything like it. And what added to the brilliance and charm of the experience was the fact that no one else, so far as he could tell, had been there with him.

He drove back to his hotel in time for the supper buffet and when he had filled his tray he looked for a table where he might find some people to tell about what he had just witnessed. He quickly chose a four-top where three women sat--two college-age girls and what turned out to be their mother. All were attractive, but what drew him was his eagerness to report his discovery to fellow tourists. "May I join you?" he asked and hadn't quite pulled his chair to the table when he blurted out, "Have you heard of the wild parakeets of Aruba? They are an amazing sight--and sound. You must not miss them. How long will you be here?"

The women blinked, looked around at one another, not quite rolling their eyes, and the older one smiled and said, "Tell us about it."

He caught his breath, slowed his heartbeat and breathing, and shook his head at this uncharacteristic display of emotional energy. Introductions followed. They were, after all, mother and two daughters, the girls on break from the University of Wisconsin at Madison, their mother along with them, not as chaperone but as fellow-traveler. Far from twins but only a year and a half apart, Heather was a junior, brunette and brown-eyed; Helen a strawberry blond sophomore; both were engagingly pretty and energetic, laughing at his attempts at wit, and just as attractively open-minded as UWM women were cracked up to be. Their mother, Jeanne, was, he thought, just as pretty, with darker hair and complexion, but with a sense of sadness in her eyes that belied the kindly smiles of her manner.

Once they had all recovered from Keith's sudden burst of bird-excitement, they had relaxed into general and generally upbeat conversation that took them through dinner and for a postprandial cocktail at the tiki bar. At no time during the two hours they spent together as a foursome did he feel uncomfortable or that they may have seemed an odd grouping to anyone else. They were clearly not a family of four, despite the age disparities, but they seemed to carry on like a group of friends. When Jeanne excused herself, saying she was tired and needed an early bedtime, he stood and offered to walk her back to their cabin. She declined, and he thought he might retire by himself; but the Gordon sisters together insisted that he stay and have another drink with them.

They clearly had something to say to him, and he was pleased to be an audience for whatever these charming young women had to say--even when the subject of their enthusiasm became clear. They wanted to tell him their mother's story, in part to account for why they were traveling with her when they could be having a high old time with their sorority sisters in Cancun. It was a regular sister act, with a version of call-and-response narrative, and he later couldn't separate what part each told; he could only reconstruct it as a coherent and unbroken narrative.

Their parents had been married for twenty-five years when Helen started college. They had hosted a gala Silver Wedding celebration for two hundred friends and family, at which their dad had given an elaborate toast to his "bride" for a quarter century of wedded bliss and the support and devotion that had boosted him to the great family and extensive successes he had enjoyed. Later that night, when the honored couple was preparing for bed, Dad told Mom that it had been a wonderful twenty-five years--but that he wanted to go in a different direction.

Next day he moved out, stunning all of those two hundred friends and family and leaving a bewildered wife who had had not the slightest inkling of any problem in, not to mention end of term for, the marriage. Jeanne had grieved at the loss but bravely faced the reality of it and maintained her composure while coping with the increased responsibilities of single-parenting. A couple months of counseling helped, in which she adopted the mantra that her therapist offered: "I am not diminished." All their friends stood by her, which helped, and the girls carried on as if nothing had harmed them, even when Dad soon began accompanying a younger woman around the social scene of Milwaukee.

In other words, they had all refused to cast a pall of tragedy around the dramatic change in their domestic lives. Except for their little brother, who brooded without tears but withdrew into a thirteen-year-old's version of clinical depression. And then little Timmy, the apple of Mom's eye and precious pet of his sisters, was killed by a hit-and-run driver while riding his bike delivering morning newspapers in their neighborhood.

Again, family and friends rallied around Mom, who this time was hardly consolable. Until Dad tried to come home. Playing the part of guilt-ridden penitent, he pleaded to be taken back into the fold, only to be turned away by Jeanne. Her feelings were consumed by anger, and she refused to assume once again the burden of nourishing Dad's shaken ego. Aroused to justifiable rage at him, she seemed to process her grief more appropriately.

Keith took all of this in, trying all the while to empathize with the doubly traumatized woman, whose presence he had found attractive and could now admire in a richer context. Meanwhile, throughout the narrative it became clearer to him that these pretty co-eds were campaigning for him to take a romantic interest in their mom. Shaking his head at how they portrayed Mom's devastated state, he wondered aloud how he might possibly bring some lightness into her blues.

We could see that you were attracted to her, they both said in collaborative ways, why don't you act on that attraction? We'll be here three more days.

"I have some problems with that," he said. "I'm here because I needed some time alone to process the end of a serious relationship, not to distract myself with a new interest. Second, I'm not sure your

Mom would welcome such attention and not feel that I was trying to take advantage of her neediness. Besides, if anything were to come of it, how would it overcome the enormous obstacles of long-distance relationships?"

Heather laughed at that, saying, "We're not trying to play eHarmony," and Helen added, "We'd just like to see her begin to re-engage in some kind of social life, to be herself and be out there." Then they both contributed a flattering argument: Mom seemed to find him kind and interesting.

"You mean 'kind of interesting?'" he said. "Well, you're kind and generous daughters and thanks for the compliment. I'll give it some thought and I'm sure we'll see each other at least in passing before we leave the island."

Truth be told, he had already given some thought to trying to make more of his chance meeting with the Gordon women, especially to make some sort of approach to Jeanne. Now, besides finding her charmingly attractive he felt more strongly drawn to her as the sad heroine of a tear-jerking tale. Besides, he'd been thinking that it was time in his life to connect with a woman his own age. Relaxing in his hot tub before going to bed, he identified an issue that he had often faced: if he didn't take advantage of the opportunity he had been offered, wouldn't he regret it?

Then he reran the negatives he had listed to the daughters and added the one about not wanting to be embarrassed by adding to his roster of rejections. And he went to sleep with the conclusion that he would try to avoid contact with "the Gordon girls" next day. It was the day he'd decided to remove another item on his Aruba bucket list, anyway, and in the early afternoon he drove over to the Marriott to try his hand at the tables. As always, those hours passed quickly, though he had kept to modest action, first losing a little at roulette, then winning a little more at blackjack, and finally trying his hand at the craps table where he went up and down, up and down, in more but milder waves than he'd ever encounter in the Caribbean waters. He stayed in the unimpressive casino for an equally unimpressive dinner and retired early without even a stop at the tiki bar.

Next morning, reading in the shade of his shack, he was surprised to see Jeanne Gordon approaching his beach chair. "I was hoping to find you," she said. "I've been thinking about those birds you saw, Keith, and wondered if you'd take me to see them later."

All his reservations went right out his glassless window. "I'd be delighted. And may I take you from there to dinner? I've heard of a good little place over on that side of the island."

The birds repeated their ritual performance, this time with an awed audience of two, and it was doubly appreciated. They shook their heads over the absence of any other interested spectators, and Keith said, "I'm so glad you asked me to do this. I'd begun to think I had dreamed the whole thing."

The evening proceeded as in a dream. They lingered over a surprisingly good dinner, drained a pitcher of sangria, and walked hand in hand along the beach when they got back to their hotel. They shared some secrets as they told tales of their lives, spoke lightly of the pleasures they still partook of in their early middle age, and they breathed deeply in the tropical atmosphere. At her cabin he embraced her, exchanging a deep kiss as if destined for fulfillment.

"I haven't been kissed like that for a long time," she said, "years before Tom left me."

"He should never have stopped. And you will yet be kissed again and again."

"Thank you, Keith," she said, turning away. "Will I see you tomorrow?"

"Of course, but bitter-sweetly, it being our last day in paradise."

Indeed, they spent all day together, talking and talking, just talking, Heather and Helen happy to leave them to it. They exchanged addresses, promising to keep in touch, and he hugged all three of them before they left for the airport, just a few hours before his own departure.

Keith thought it best to let Jeanne initiate any correspondence and didn't obsess over it when two weeks passed. Then he dropped her a brief note, asking how she was doing and casually mentioning how much he'd enjoyed meeting them all. This time the response was prompt and warm. "I've been thinking about you a lot," she wrote. "It's too bad there's a thousand miles between us, when I guess there could be much more to draw us together."

The pace of the exchange quickened, though for some reason neither one initiated a phone call (not to mention "phone sex," as Keith occasionally thought). You could hardly have called them love-notes anyway. And then on Valentine's Day he received a small package in the mail--one of those little red heart-shaped tin containers usually filled with candy mints with amorous lettering inscribed on top. Inside this one, however, was just a folded slip of paper: "This coupon is redeemable for one fun-filled weekend (of your choice) in Milwaukee."

Keith read it three times before he was sure that the parenthetical phrase referred to the calendar and not the kind of fun that might fill their time together. Then he realized that in just two weeks it would be Sadie Hawkins Day, falling on a Friday this year, and that's when he picked up the phone. The second call was to Jeanne. He told her that he was thrilled by her message and that he could get an afternoon flight to Milwaukee, appropriately since she had asked him, on February 29th.

They spoke once more a week later so that he could get an idea of what clothes he'd need for whatever she had planned. She said they might want to go for a run, weather permitting, that he needn't bring anything to dress for church Sunday morning because she didn't expect him to attend Mass with her, and that otherwise casual was the word though they'd be joining some of her friends for dinner at their country club Saturday night. He didn't ask what had led to her surprise invitation.

She told him anyway, in the Peugeot on the way home from the airport. She had been thinking of him, she said, ever since Aruba and wondering if they'd ever meet again, and then, after she had signed her divorce papers, she decided to take matters into her own hands. Tom's young girlfriend, as it happened, had tired of him, rejected him, and moved to Denver where he had taken her on a business trip and she'd become enamored of the twenty-something-thirty-something lifestyle they had encountered there.

Tom had then begged Jeanne again to take him back and destroy those papers, besieging her with blooming bouquets of superfluous flowers and mawkish, drunken phone calls. "Not on your life," she had told him and in her quiet but firm voice said that if he didn't stop stalking her she would get a protective order from their friend Judge Daley. He understood that she meant it--and she knew it was time for her to start really living her own new life.

In the comfortable old-brick colonial, a fire had already been set in the living room and she had prepared a dinner of mountain trout while the complementary chardonnay had been chilling. Everything else was comfortably warm, including the music she had chosen, the rug in front of the fireplace, and the gradual but sure approach to their love-making. Keith had never enjoyed foreplay so much; it was at the same time calming and arousing. They seemed to fit perfectly together, responding to each other with gestures of mutual appreciation and acceptance and generosity. She was sweetness and firmness, and he told her in every natural and spontaneous way he could of his admiration. He felt blessed--lifted and gifted--and wondered how any man in his right mind could have walked away from this lovely woman.

The weather was clear and windless on Saturday, so they went for a run together (something they had both neglected to do in Aruba), matching strides as if they were regular training partners, four miles in just over forty minutes. Then they showered together, taking unapologetic pleasure in each other's bodies, and went back to bed for "afternoon delights."

The evening was a smashing success, although Keith had had some misgivings at being the stranger among the three other couples who were Jeanne's (and had been Tom's) closest friends. The women played golf and bridge together, the four families had traditional barbecue gatherings on holidays (thirteen children among them until the tragic loss of Timmy Gordon), and the four men had a standing tee time in good weather after they had all gone to church together. In winter the families would trek up to Bemidji to the ski resorts of Buena Vista. Same church, same country club, a shared life. Well, the men had found a new fourth, having without discussion dismissed Tom from their foursome and, for that matter, from their lives.

Keith soon felt comfortable with them all. They accepted him graciously, and he appreciated the effortless ways they all showed their love for Jeanne. An interesting mix in their own right, all with ethnic Catholic backgrounds--German, French, Irish, Italian, and Polish, but with no one couple sharing a national origin, a little melting-pot European union all its own. Successful men, all three (accountant, automobile dealer, realtor) but modestly comfortable in their own skin, attentive husbands and active fathers; the women all involved in clubs and civic activities, appreciative of their men, and devoted to their intimate group.

They were all fans of the Packers and Marquette basketball, and welcomed some good-natured kidding from Keith (with his NFL knowledge and the stories he told about Al McGuire). Of politics and religion there was no talk, and they all found ways to include him in whatever group-speak occurred. Best of all, they made an effort to show their approval of his connection with Jeanne, though he thought they would do the same for anyone their dear friend would bring into the group.

Jeanne went to early Mass on Sunday, leaving Keith to work the Sunday Times puzzles. And then she produced a prodigious brunch for both of them. They took their time to enjoy it all, then retired to the bedroom ditto. In fact they stretched it out so long that they had to rush for him to catch his plane. They said their goodbyes in the car, a somewhat awkward embrace in which he thanked her for a wonderful weekend and she said, "Thank *you*--it was perfect, all I hoped it would be." He slid his carry-on out of the car, looked over his shoulder as he went through the door toward the security line, and saw that Jeanne's Peugeot was already in the exit lane.

He daydreamed the flight away, reliving the heady experience. He had been drawn to the woman by her story and found extraordinary beauty in her person. Somehow he felt as if he'd traveled that route before. And now he composed her future in his mind. A happy ending. She had left school after her sophomore year to become a nineteen-year-old homemaker and now would go back to finish a degree in Art History. She had already enrolled in summer school, and she was also working part-time in a travel agency. There was no future in that, she knew, and might consider real estate or some sort of happy-making work, like catering or party-planning, if she couldn't find an opening in the Art Museum. Graduate work in Chicago at the Art Institute? Well, a girl could dream. Maybe a partnership in a gallery was more likely.

She'd sell the house and downsize into a townhouse, without leaving her parish, designing a home for her eclectic taste. She'd still worship, golf, play bridge, and go skiing with her crowd; and she'd keep running as long as her knees allowed. The girls would go on to grad school, Heather on her way to the bar, Helen on hers to a veterinarian practice. Both would marry happily, but not until near thirty, and would make Jeanne a doting grandmother of four, two named Timmy among them.

She would remarry happily, till death would them part. The tagline was this: she and Keith would never see each other again. He would always feel blessed at having known her and played a role in her story--as pivot or game-changer or turning point or maybe launching pad. Before his plane had taxied to the gate, he realized that she had done the same for him.

Acknowledgments

My thanks to my brother Phil who passed along his admiration for Billie (and many others) and was ever my most constructive reader. "The Man Who Touched Billie" was runner-up in the *Potomac Review* Short Story Contest 2002-03. My thanks to the staff.

"Collared" was runner-up in the F. Scott Fitzgerald Short Story Contest in 2004. My thanks to the late Alan Cheuse, that year's judge for the contest, whose voice on NPR had always been worth hearing.

My brother never wanted to see "Payback" in print, but in elegiac tribute, I thank him yet again for "his" story.

"Up from Ashes, Down from Speed," along with "Sophie" and "They Were the Fiedlers," are indebted to the superb copy-editing of my grandson Mickey Isaacs.

"Elevator" was inspired by its namesake by Robert Coover. I regret our respective times at Brown did not overlap.

"Zero-Grounded" began with my conviction, post 9/11, that the actual totality of losses in major calamities would never be fully numbered. RIP.

Many thanks to my crew of guides through the Archway process, the efficient and respectful relay team of Virginia Morrel, Stephanie Frame, Kayla Stobaugh, and Kelly Martin.

About the Author

Neil D. Isaacs holds degrees from Dartmouth, UC Berkeley, Brown, and UMAB School of Social Work. He was a college professor for forty years, a psychotherapist for twenty years, and a writer throughout. His hundreds of credits include newspaper columns (Washington Post, Boston Globe, New York Times, Baltimore Sun), magazine and journal pieces, and three dozen books. He lives with his wife in Pompano Beach, Florida.

Made in the USA
Middletown, DE
12 January 2018